I0552013

FUTURE BE DAMNED

Last Hope #5

REBECCA ROYCE

The unauthorized reproduction or distribution of a copyrighted work is illegal. Criminal copyright infringement, including infringement without monetary gain, is investigated by the FBI and is punishable by fines and federal imprisonment.

Please purchase only authorized electronic editions and do not participate in, or encourage, the electronic piracy of copyrighted materials. Your support of the author's rights is appreciated.

This book is a work of fiction. Names, characters, places, and incidents are the products of the author's imagination or used fictitiously. Any resemblance to actual events, locales or persons, living or dead, is entirely coincidental.

Future Be Damned (Last Hope #5)

Copyright @ 2018 by Rebecca Royce

Ebook ISBN: 978-1-947672-59-8

Print ISBN: 978-1-947672-60-4

Cover art by Lyn Forester

Content Editing: Heather Long

Copy/Proofread Editing: Jennifer at Bookends Editing

Formatting: Ripley Proserpina

All rights reserved. Except for use in any review, the reproduction or utilization of this work, in whole or in part, in any form by any electronic, mechanical or other means now known or hereafter invented, is forbidden without the written permission of the publisher.

Published by Rebecca Royce

www.rebeccaroyce.com

🏵 Created with Vellum

This book is dedicated to anyone who has ever had to pull themselves out of the mud and say to the universe that today isn't the day they are falling on their face. Literally or Figuratively. Aspen and I are right there with you. —RR

PREFACE

And so it shall be that four shall be chosen and from the Sisterhood they will rise. The hopes and dreams of the entire universe will rise up with them. They shall win or we all shall perish.

—From the book of Esma, in the Dawn of our Lady, from a time long ago but not forgotten.

ASPEN

The taste of mud in my mouth made me gag. For a second, I wondered if after all the trouble I'd been through to survive, all of the years of pushing myself to the outer limits of what was possible, if I was going to choke to death on some mud, lying flat on my stomach, unable to pick up my head off the ground. My muscles shook from the effort of trying.

Rain pounded on my back, hitting my exposed skin where my shirt had ridden up, leaving me at the unforgiving mercy of the elements as the weather itself seemed to taunt me.

Get up, Aspen. Get up or die here. Get up.

I didn't speak weather, but if I did, I would swear that was what it said to me. In the not too far distance, the sounds of impending doom, also known as the horde of demon controlled zombies, headed straight for me. I had to get off this ground. I yelled my frustration, finally managing to wrench my head up. I spit, hard, forcing the mud out of my mouth.

I was not dying today.

With another shout, I dragged my body to a sitting position and then to my feet. Sister Krystal had sacrificed herself for me, giving me her powers before she vanished from the world, likely forever. She'd believed that my role as the Warrior was more important than anything she had yet to do, and without so much as asking me what I thought about that, she'd done it. My cells took in the Sisterhood power, the magic that all those like me shared, as I tried to become what I always should have been. I stood in the rain alone wondering how this could be happening.

I lifted my head and bellowed to the clouds, to divinity, to anyone who wanted to listen. How in all that was sweet and good in the world was I supposed to do this? I'd had my powers taken from me before I was born in this body. I'd never had to manage them before as a human, and I didn't have the slightest idea how to use them.

I couldn't be anyone's savior. I couldn't even stand up straight.

I limped forward, practically dragging my left leg behind me. I'd fit right in with the mass of the dead coming to kill anyone in their path. Things had been slightly better lately in this area, since Krystal had worked her incredible powers and revitalized nature. She'd also taken out Katrina. Why in all things holy would she give up her powers and give them to me when she'd so obviously been the most powerful Sister ever born?

I cried out my frustration as I almost tripped and went down again. I couldn't let that happen. I might never have gotten up again.

Lightning lit up the sky followed by a crash of thunder. I was so wet I couldn't get any worse, but I still pulled myself toward the house. I'd been raised here as a plain old human. No Sister had come for me as a baby to take me away to the Sisterhood. The Oracle had not seen my birth; the Prophet saw no futures with me in it because I had no powers.

Or I hadn't until a few minutes ago. I stared down at my hands. They burned like a million needles assaulted the tips of my fingers. Why did there have to be so much pain? Babies were born powerful. Shouldn't my body just absorb the powers like I'd always had them?

I didn't know what caught my attention or stopped my walk to the house, but I turned around. I wiped my hair out of my face, pushing it aside. It sloshed back down, and I did it a second time. I stared at the sky. The lightning flashed again. Then I registered what I saw. Above my head, five black ravens flew through the storm. They came toward me like they were honed to do so and perhaps they were. If I was a Sister then they were my guards.

The trouble was guards weren't ravens anymore. They didn't fly. I'd no sooner thought it than, as if on cue with my thoughts and the thunder ringing in my ears, they fell from the sky. All five of them in different directions. As if they'd instantly lost the ability to soar, they plummeted to the ground.

My body went numb a second before my brain stuttered. Breath left my body. I knew those five men. Or I had known them in another dimension. Most people couldn't remember if they'd ever lived before, had another life. That was normal. In fact, I didn't know if they had. But Sisters were set up to come here before they were born. With a little help, we could remember that time. When they'd taken my Sister abilities from me, they hadn't ridden me of those memories.

So I knew who those five birds really were....

I'd known them forever.

I'd loved them. Once.

It had been a very long time since we'd had anything to do with one another. Tears sprang to my eyes. I hadn't glimpsed them as birds since I'd been born. We hadn't been allowed to see each other at all. And yet I knew them on sight. As I always would.

Reed... dark like the clothes he'd always worn. He was so adept at fighting that he'd been charged with teaching everyone else. He'd have been number One of my guards if things had gone correctly. He'd taken the blame for what happened, even though it had really been my fault.

Alexander... blond hair, dark eyes—so dark they were almost black—that fell in direct contrast to the lightness of his hair. He was in a constant battle with himself about the right thing to do and was often falling into arguments with Reed. They almost never agreed. He'd been set to be my number Two.

Stone... so blond, he was often called pretty because of the gentleness of his features and the light blue of his eyes. His personality negated anyone using that term for very long. Like his name, he had lots of sharp edges and he could wound. He never acted that way with me. There had never been anyone more careful with my feelings than Stone. I was the only one left out of his temper when it rose.

Jamie... black haired, strong, bulky. He was like a sweet battering ram. The only of my guards I had ever seen cry, he was never afraid of his emotions. He wore them on his sleeve. He was gallant, believed in true love. He'd been the one who liked to cuddle, to hug. But he was lethal. He cut down demons without thought and never looked back or questioned his role in the fight.

Gage... red-headed with green eyes. Clever to a fault. He was often the reason anything got done, quietly seeing to it. I used to think I couldn't get through a day without making eye contact with Gage just to see to it that the world was settled. I'd know in his eyes that all was okay. Now I knew that I could, but it would be miserable.

I shouted at the sky. They'd all fallen, losing their ability to fly all at once. The first time I'd seen them with my human eyes. Twenty-four years of silence. And now... they were just dead? Why do this to me? Why give me these powers my body obviously couldn't manage and make me watch my loves die?

Part of me considered just sinking into the mud, just letting this all go. Enough was sometimes enough. Except I wasn't built that way. At my very core, I was a fighter, always had been, and I couldn't give up now. I just had to get my legs working.

A sound caught my attention. What now? I tried to spin around and almost fell over again. I was worse than a toddler learning to walk. At this rate, I was getting nowhere fast. Those five men had once meant the world to me. There were too many misunderstandings and things said in anger to take back at this point. We'd never have our forever in love that some of the other Sisters got. Still, I wouldn't leave them to die alone on the ground any more than they'd have done that to me.

If only I could physically get there.

A horse ran to my side. I blinked. A silver-gray horse, fully saddled, stared at me like I should know her. That was a strange thought. I didn't really know what the horse was thinking. Did I? I didn't really know what powers I had. Damn it, this was all really confusing.

Did Sisters communicate with horses?

She neighed at me before stomping her feet.

I touched her side. She was silky, not at all how I'd expected her to feel. She pushed against me. Okay, she must not have hated that I'd touched her. I hadn't even given it any thought, and I was lucky I didn't get my hand bitten off. I'd never been this close to a horse before.

She made a sound that resembled a huff and got down on her knees. I stared at her. Did she want me to get on her back? I couldn't have mounted her if she'd stayed upright. This was... odd. I wasn't sure I'd figure out how to stay upright.

The sounds of the zombies in the distance increased. My thoughts were a jumble as I tried to process everything that had happened.

"You can't be just a horse. You're somehow related to all of this, aren't you? I mean, the guys are birds here. You're something. I just don't know what. The question is are you a good horse or a bad horse?" I had to speak aloud. I had to hear my own voice to center me. "Or maybe that's a dumb question. Why would the demons send me a horse when they have a mob about to descend on me and I'm helpless?"

I managed to wrench myself forward and somehow get onto the saddle. It wasn't pretty. I didn't hurt the horse, I didn't think. She stood, me on her back. How did I even know she was a she? Is this what happened to Sisters? Did random things just take place with them? I'd been so busy trying to help from the sidelines I'd failed to pay any attention to these kinds of details.

I held onto the reins—I at least knew enough to do that —and she took off running. I didn't know what to call her. Did horses have names?

The rain pelted us both, and it might have been my imagination, but it seemed to get harder. The horse ran, and I held on for dear life. My already hurting body jolted with every step, and I cried out, hoping I didn't fall off and make the situation worse.

Eventually, we entered the woods closest to my house. As a child I'd run here to get away from my brutal mother. When divinity sent me down as a human they hadn't given me an ideal childhood. Not that anyone had one, it was the end of days after all, but my mother had been a raving lunatic. She wasn't even possessed. I couldn't blame her brand of nasty on the demons. She'd just been a horror show all on her own.

The horse came to a sudden stop, and I managed to stay upright. Where were we? I looked around. Lying on the ground, in his human form, was Reed. He was out cold. In his signature black, he almost blended into the ground. All the guards wore all black, but Reed had chosen to do it even when he didn't have to. Between the rain, the upcoming night, and the trees, we were surrounded by darkness.

I stumbled off the horse. She needed a name. I was going to have to come up with one. But that didn't matter right then. My legs buzzed with every movement, but they worked. Was he dead? I got over to Reed with just that thought in my mind. I touched him. He was warm and his pulse steady. I let go of the breath I held. He could still be very hurt, but he wasn't dead. Where were the others?

Not far from Reed, Gage lay in a similar position. I did my best to rush to him. He was also alive. Then Alexander. Stone. Jamie. They all breathed. I needed them to be closer to one another if I was going to help them. Moving was hard but adjusting them without making things worse? Could I do it?

I tugged on Jamie to see if he would go. He wouldn't. I slumped down onto the ground, finding a middle spot between them. This was going to have to do. Drops of rain still came through the trees, but I didn't care. I looked up at the horse.

"Thanks."

She seemed to nod. Was she going to stay here with me? The world tilted left then right. I grabbed onto my head. What was happening? Dizziness assaulted me before darkness took me under.

I woke as a strong hand touched the side of my face. I blinked awake. Everything hurt and the entirety of the day hit my consciousness before I'd fully opened my eyes. Reed cupped the side of my face. His eyes were red rimmed, and smudges of dirt marred the beauty that had always been the sheer masculinity of Reed's face.

Desire to throw my arms around him warred with the knowledge that the last time Reed and I saw each other—hell, the last time I'd seen any of them—we'd said things that could never be taken back. There were some things that once uttered could never be unheard.

I'd thrown as many barbs at them as they had at me.

I breathed heavy, like I'd just run a great distance.

"Aspen." His voice was so low. I'd forgotten the sound of it. "You're okay. I thought... you were so still. I thought maybe you were dead."

"I..." I struggled upright. "I hurt everywhere. But I didn't fall from the sky so... yeah. I have no room to complain right now."

He sucked in a breath. "How are we all here? I don't..."

He didn't get to finish his question. Alexander was suddenly right next to him. He shot Reed a look I couldn't read before turning to stare at me. "You okay, baby? Are you hurt? It worked."

"Worked?" Reed shook his head. "What worked? What is happening?"

"We fixed it." Alexander took my hand and kissed it. "Right before you were all sent down we tried to set a plan in motion. It wasn't working. There was one last chance. It happened."

Reed reared back. "Why didn't you tell me about this plan?"

"Because you'd have stopped it." Stone elbowed into my vision on the other side of Reed. "You'd already made yourself clear where you stood on following the directive. We weren't going to let you report it. Aspen, you're okay? Thank divinity. I wasn't sure I'd see this day."

I blinked at Stone. His beautiful, usually pretty face, was scarred. One jagged line marred the skin on the left side. "What happened to you?" I tried to sit up more. It took more effort than I'd have liked. I wasn't better yet.

"Demon." He shrugged. "It's dead. I'm scarred. I don't care unless you do."

"How did you engage with a demon?" The birds never did. "And..."

Jamie arrived in the picture. He let out an audible breath. "I had started to not believe it. I was losing hope. When Krystal wasn't falling into play, I thought for sure we had lost our last best hope at this happening."

His words jarred me back into reality right as Gage came over, not squatting down but looking at me from above.

"Krystal?" I had to ask. I was as confused as Reed.

"That's right." Gage put his hands on his hips. "We pushed Krystal to do what she had to do. To be where she had to be. To be in the path of those who would give her a second chance at life so she could turn her powers over to you. There was one remote path where that happened. We took the vision away from those who might see it and made sure that happened. We did that. For you."

Reed winced, dropping back on his behind. "You can't just go around fucking with divinity."

He so rarely used profanity. Or at least that used to be the case. I rose on shaky legs. "Let me see if I've got this straight. Four of you schemed to undo what divinity declared in order to get me powers? To the point that Krystal and her guards are now dead?"

Reed rubbed his eyes. "I was suddenly compelled to shift and come to you. To fly. Then I lost the ability. It was all very... primal."

I addressed Gage when I spoke. He was the schemer. I knew this about him. "Gage?"

"Yes, we did, my love. We did because having your powers taken from you was a huge mistake. Ours, not yours. And only you can save us all. Even if Reed is too pigheaded to see it. Also, we're selfish. I'm not going through eternity without you. If you're a Sister, I'm one of your guards. That's how it works."

My temper flared. It had always been brutal and probably my worst trait. "Krystal is dead."

Power surged out of me, skirting a tree across from us and exploding a rock. I gaped, slipping backward and falling into the tree. Everything hurt. What had happened? I wasn't a crier, I really never had been, but I wiped two tears from the corners of my eyes before I could stop myself.

"You okay?" Stone touched my forehead. "She's burning up."

"Her body isn't used to what's happening to her." Reed grabbed me. "We have to get her cooled down. Sisters take years to adjust to their powers. They come in segments, not all at once, and they do it in Sisterhoods with experts around them to help. This has to be hell on her."

Alexander nodded at Reed, taking my hand. "This way."

What did they propose doing? Cooling me down wasn't exactly an easy task, and we weren't near any herbs that might help with that.

"Raise your arms," Jamie told me, and even though that seemed an odd request, I did as he asked. He slipped my shirt over my head, exposing me to the elements. Rain pelted down at me from a space in between the trees. It wasn't pleasant.

"Pants," Gage told me, and I let them pull them off of me. I was in my underwear, getting soaked, and I didn't care at all.

My long black hair stuck to my body, too wet to do anything but just let it be.

The guys were all so tall. I'd always been tiny, in every existence. Tiny but strong. I didn't feel that way now. Weakness was my middle name or maybe my only name. I'd always been fine with tolerating it in other people, never myself. My own worst enemy, Sister Superior, had told me once about myself.

My knees quaked. "I can't stay upright."

"Sshh," Reed whispered. "We've got you. We'll keep you upright. The rain is just cooling you down so you don't take out any other unsuspecting rocks."

I laughed, despite the circumstances. He was funny. I'd forgotten that. Alexander ran a hand down my back. "Krystal was already dead. Had been a long time. She'd never have found her guys if we hadn't helped direct Beelzebub toward her."

That didn't make this better. "I don't know if I even want to know what the four of you did, how far into the hole you went on this. That woman didn't deserve to have her life or death messed with for me. The planet is coming back to life because of her. She should still be here."

"Aspen," Reed spoke again. "I didn't know about it either. What's done is done. We can debate what they should and shouldn't have maneuvered another time. For now, why don't you just let us take care of you? We were never going to get to be your guards. It's been an ache for all of us. An emptiness. Our love for you continues to be the driving force behind why we exist. I don't have to have spoken to them in twenty-four years to know that all five of us feel that way. Just be. For a few minutes. Calm down."

I really wished I could. "Reed, there is so much that can't be undone. You know that, right? We can't take any of that back?"

"I wish you'd let me." Gage's voice shook. "I need to offer you my deepest apologies, Aspen. Not for Krystal. She'd never have gotten to do any of that stuff if she'd just been left to die at the hands of the Darkness. No, for the Before Time. For what happened and the role I played. Reed did what he did but none of that could have happened if not for me."

He spoke of the moments when we'd all fallen apart, when thinking to save me, to save all of us, Reed had sacrificed himself. When he'd left us. And I'd become a Sister without five guards and therefore not a Sister at all.

My body was officially cold. Not from the rain. From the memories.

2

BEFORE

I hurried along the path to the meeting place. It wasn't every day that Sister Superior summoned me, and I wasn't going to be late. I passed others on the way. The one they called Anne, her light bright, nodded at me. Her guards surrounded her. They were always laughing. Teagan walked with other Sisters, all of them bright and strong. In the distance I could see Mika throwing energy with a woman they called Krystal; they chatted with Beth as they practiced their abilities. All of them had guards of some kind, some of them men, some of them women. Love was love. It was all beautiful. And we needed all of it to beat back the evil that was coming.

I didn't have guards yet. Maybe I never would. Sister Superior had to match you with five souls, destined for you, people who would stay with you through the fight. I was strong. Everyone said so. And yet I had no soul mates. The idea bothered me at night when I lay alone, not listening to the sounds of love around me.

"Aspen." Sister Superior turned as I entered. She'd have known I was coming for a long time. Her powers were immense. It amazed me she had to speak at all. She might actually know what was going to come out of our mouths at all times. "Do you know why I summoned you?"

I was afraid I did. "I blew it up again. The demon. I know that I'm not supposed to do that. I don't mean to. When I get really worked up, things just... go that way. I apologize. I will work on my technique for as long as it takes to not disgrace you."

She waved her hand. "You don't disgrace me. Ever. What concerns me is what I think I have to do to you."

There were stories about this. "You'll send me away. No battle. I'm not fit to help."

"Oh, Aspen." She embraced me. "No. You're so far off on this one. I'm introducing you to your guards today. If you like them, they'll be with you, always. Even when you become the Warrior."

Joy rushed through me, followed by a cold dread so powerful it stopped me short like I'd been frozen in ice for eternity. The Warrior? She who prophecy foretold would end the great evil. She was pivotal to the battle. Oh everyone had roles. We all had titles. They mattered little save for a few key ones. Sister Superior down below, the one who would run the true Sisterhood. The Oracle, she who could see the Sisters born. The Prophet, she who would see the future. The Crone, the wise teacher who would remember that which was forgotten first. The Healer who could put things right again. The Love Giver. The Compassionate One.

There were hundreds of them.

The Warrior killed the Evil One. The worst demon. The one who made all of this happen. She fought and she battled. She either won or she vanished forever.

Her soul would be gone. She would not be reunited in an afterlife. She wouldn't have an afterlife. If she lost, she'd be gone.

I rubbed the back of my neck. "Sister, I am not strong enough."

Sister Superior put her hand on my shoulder. "You are more than strong enough. You are by far the strongest Sister I've ever taught. You will destroy him. I know you will." She turned. "And you won't be alone. There are five men who have been waiting for you. Bothering me to no end. They're not supposed to, but these five don't always do as they're told. I told them they had to wait. They just had to until you'd finished training. You get a break now. Then you go." Sister Superior touched her finger to her mouth. "One thing. It's a lot to ask. Don't tell them you're the Warrior."

I blinked. Soul mates weren't supposed to keep secrets from each other. Were they? "Why not?"

"They won't like it. There is enough pressure. They don't need to know just how much. You can handle this. You won't even remember the title when you go there anyway. You'll just do what has to be done."

I hoped she was right. I wasn't at all certain about any of this. The Warrior? Lying? She embraced me, a strange move for Sister Superior.

"Come."

I followed her from the room outside to where the guards sparred. They were always practicing if they weren't with their Sisters. They never could be sharp enough, strong enough. But there were just five outside right now.

My heart sputtered. It was *them*. Among ourselves, as potential Sisters, we watched the guards. How could we not? And I hadn't been able to stop watching these five, but I wasn't alone in that. Reed. Alexander. Stone. Jamie. Gage. No one bested them, ever. They were strong. They argued, a lot, but they stood together against the others. I loved to listen to them laugh. They always seemed to be able to find the joy in things.

"You like them." She didn't phrase that as a question.

"Did you pick them for *me*?" I couldn't believe it. There were better souls than me. I might be the Warrior but I was also always screwing things up. I didn't believe the five of them would want to put up with that for eternity.

She didn't answer me, instead whistling loud enough that she caught the attention of the five men sparring on the field. They all stopped what they were doing and instantly came to attention. Not one of them moved.

"I think I've been promising you I would make a match for some time now with a specific woman that you've been pestering me about." She motioned toward me. "If you can win her, she's yours."

If they could win me? Did she think there was a chance I was going to say no? One second they were in their human forms, balls of light glowing around them, and the next they were birds. Five of them. In front of me. Then just as fast they were men again.

They all spoke at once as Sister Superior nodded at me before backing up. All thoughts of what I shouldn't tell them fled. They were mine? Reed, Alexander, Stone, Jamie, and Gage were mine? I tried to answer their rapid-fire questions, my mind a whirlwind.

"Stop," Reed called out. "We're overwhelming her. We're gentlemen. We know how to do better than this." He cleared his throat. "Sister Aspen, it is our utmost pleasure to meet you today. To formally meet you. We've been... hoping you were ours. For some time. If you'd have us."

I swallowed. "Forgive me, I have no experience talking to men." They all looked at each other, small grins on their faces. Was what I'd just said ridiculous? "As is evidenced by the fact that I just said that?"

I looked down. I might be the Warrior. Give me a demon any day over this.

"Hey." Alexander tapped my chin, and I lifted it. "We have no experience talking to women. We like to watch you fight. You're so strong. The strongest out there. You're so beautiful. Especially then. I am in awe of your ability."

Stone grinned broadly. "We stay up talking about you."

"And we really hoped we'd at least get a chance to tell you," Jamie took my hand and kissed it. "When Sister Superior said you were ours, that we just had to wait, we thought we might perish from the effort."

Gage took my other hand and squeezed it. "We hope you didn't have others in mind."

Was he kidding? "No, of course not. I'd... I'd like to give this a go."

HAD IT ONLY BEEN MONTHS SINCE I'D BEEN MATCHED WITH them? Time slipped away in this place. It might have been years. I lay on the ground, staring up at the sky next to Reed. He pointed at a cloud. "That one. I think that one looks like a dove."

He might have been right, but he was more imaginative than me. I didn't see things like that as easily. I had seen how one resembled a boat earlier. I loved how he smelled. Was the weird? I rolled over to look at him closer. "You're so handsome, Reed."

His grin was fast as he also rolled over to stare directly at me, stomach-to-stomach. "You think so?"

"I do. And you know it, too. Both that I think so and that you are."

He kissed me gently on the lips. "You're beautiful. But I don't think you know that. Or you just don't care. I can't figure out which one of those things is true. Maybe both, somehow? One thing I'm looking forward to down there in the muck of things is the physical. I hear that in human bodies this," he stroked my arm, "is even more intense. I want to touch you everywhere and see."

That was hard for me to imagine. I liked how they touched me now. I loved how our souls fused together, how I could feel their light against me like the warm touch of the sun. I loved the colors our souls made when we were all together. But, yes, the contact was supposed to be better in stronger physical forms.

We'd look the same but somehow also be different. It was all very confusing, and we wouldn't understand it until we were there.

Or so I'd been told.

Jamie threw himself down on the ground, coming up behind me to nuzzle my back. He sighed, and although I couldn't see him, I'd lain with him enough to picture him with his eyes closed and the slightest smile on his face. When he spoke, it was on a whisper. "Hi, Aspen. Hi, Reed."

"Hi, Jamie," I whispered back while Reed snuggled back down on the ground. They'd been fighting all morning. They could go forever, but when they were done, they crashed. I hadn't been thinking about how tired Reed had to have been while he'd lain there and tried to get me to see the shape of clouds.

Was it wrong that I loved sleeping with them so much? Why hadn't I known the comfort of being wrapped against another soul in slumber? For the entirety of my existence, I'd missed them, and I hadn't even known it.

Somehow that made sense...

"Hey." Alexander caught my attention, and I opened my eyes to look at him. He burned the hottest out of all of them. I was convinced that was why Reed led and not him. Reed stayed steady. Alexander went up and down too much to be in charge.

I sat up. Neither Reed nor Jamie moved. "You okay?"

"They want us. It's time. The big meeting."

Gage arrived. He must have been running because he was out of breath. He leaned against Alexander. "Stone is waiting for us there. You know how he likes to get the specific row of seats."

Dread filled me deep inside. I'd never told them what Sister Superior had said and now that seemed like a huge mistake. She'd never had soul mates. Maybe even with all of her wisdom, she didn't understand exactly how this was supposed to go.

Reed got to his feet, rubbing his eyes as he went. "Do you suppose they'll let us look at the fates now? All of these months keeping everyone in the dark. The guys are all getting restless. All the teams. There's grumbling. But I heard that some people do know. They've told some of the Sisters who they are, which I find rather aggravating."

"Yeah?" Jamie kissed my back before he rose. "Who's who?"

My ears rang. "We should probably talk about this. Can someone get Stone?"

Gage took my hand, squeezing my fingers. "Anne is Sister Superior down there. Mika is the Oracle."

"Well chosen."

He was right. They were. "Guys, we need to talk."

A crowd rushed by us, someone banging into me.

Alexander whirled around. "Watch where you're going. That's my Sister you hit."

I was okay. He was always short tempered when he was tired. "It's fine. We need to talk."

Even as I said it, I knew there'd be no time. We'd reached our destination. Sister Superior stood with some of the other ancient Sisters. They were old souls who had done their time serving so long ago they'd reached a point where they were now in control of the rest of us. This was interesting because it meant they'd been through a complete cycle. They understood what happened to us after death. Well, to everyone else. If I didn't kill the Darkness, nothing was happening to me. I was just gone.

I sat down. Sister Superior began speaking. "It's time to send the souls. And as this is happening, the potential futures are starting to show themselves to us."

This had always been the hardest part for me. We were all together but some of us would arrive earlier than others in the timeline. Yet, somehow, our futures weren't set. It had to do with free will. We could screw up when we got down there and we'd likely not remember any or all of this. I sighed.

I was the Warrior. I looked at Gage. I had to say something. Right this second. I opened my mouth and closed it. This wasn't news you just dumped on someone in the middle of a meeting.

"Some of you will say yes to the Darkness." She looked away. My heart sank. Who would do that? "Some of you won't. In any case, I leave it to you now."

Wait a second. Were we going right now? I gasped. Jamie kissed my cheek. "Don't worry, love. It'll be okay."

She wasn't done speaking. "There is a chance that things are going to all go wrong down there. All of it may fall apart. That is a potential future."

Reed sighed and spoke low. "This wouldn't happen if there was an actual leader of the guards. They need someone on the ground there to do it."

Alexander nodded. "Agreed. But who's going to sign up for that? Who's going to leave their Sister to go lead?"

Reed shook his head. "It would be like living with a constant hole in your heart."

"Who would betray you, Sister Superior?" A woman named Katrina called out. She was lovely. Probably the most physically beautiful of all of us. "Why would anyone choose to do that with so much at stake?"

"The power of the Darkness is all consuming and you are being sent down without prior knowledge. That is unfortunate but that is how it has to be. We always knew when we foresaw this man becoming this creature that there would be losses. Extreme losses."

She sighed. "In that vein, let's get to it. There is no time like now. When it comes down to it, you won't remember any of this except that you will slip into your roles..."

"Sorry, Sister." Reed stood up. That didn't surprise me. He was always willing to buck tradition. "What kinds of things are going wrong?"

She waved her hand in the air. "Sit down, Reed."

As much as she admired his skill, and I could tell from how she gave him the most to do on the training field, she didn't like him. Was it just the interrupting or something else? I wasn't going to ask. I didn't want to fight with Sister Superior, and I knew I'd destroy the world for Reed. That was just how I felt about my guys.

He nodded and took his seat. "Guess she doesn't want to tell us."

Stone elbowed him. "Or she doesn't want to tell you. I bet if Thaddeus asked, she'd tell him."

The woman did seem to like Thaddeus more, even though Reed was stronger. There was something going on. I looked over at the fountain that showed her our futures. What did she see in there? What did she know? Or was I overthinking it? What would I see if I looked in there? And why did they let the man become the Darkness to begin with?

He'd been human. Made terrible decisions and eventually become the strongest evil to ever walk the planet by the sheer force of his will. Why not stop him before it happened? Why let this happen in the future at all?

If we could move through time, why do this? Those were not questions I got answers to. Instead, I was sent out to fight. That is what I was best at, and apparently I'd be doing it.

Many futures. Many pasts. Maybe there would be one where we never had to do this at all.

"The Sisters have all been told who they are. Anne will be my voice as Sister Superior. In the end, it will be Aspen who defeats him. She is the Warrior."

Next to me, all five of my guys jolted in some form.

"What?" Like Reed, Alexander wasn't any good at being quiet. "Hold on a second."

My whole body tensed. Muscles I didn't know I had hurt. "Alexander, listen..."

He jumped up. "No. We haven't agreed to this."

Reed grabbed my knee. "You knew?"

I nodded. I wasn't going to lie, even though I'd essentially been doing just that since I met them. Stone leaned forward onto his knees. "And you didn't tell us, why?"

"I was told not to." That was the answer I would have to keep giving whenever I was asked. I hated it. Even the words tasted bad in my mouth, sour and bitter at the same time.

Jamie's face fell into utter horror. "You've been keeping this from us? Lying this whole time? You didn't trust us? Who told you to do this? By divinity, who are you?"

As though I'd just become a stranger to him. We were supposed to be sharing our souls. He was right. I'd kept a huge portion of it back. "Jamie..."

Sister Superior watched us closely. In fact, all eyes were on us. "I see that she did as she was told and didn't tell you. I told her not to."

"Why would you do that?" Reed never had trouble yelling at her. "Don't you think that would have been useful for us to know?"

Bryant, Anne's number One, rose. "Maybe we should table this for another time."

"There is no more time. You're all leaving now. It's happening." Sister Superior shook her head.

No, it couldn't be like this. We couldn't have these feelings before we went off to battle. "Can I just have a minute?"

"She's strong but she's not strong enough." Alexander shook his head. "She's not going to win this. We know what happens to the Warrior if she loses. We've all read the prophecies. You knew we would stop this and that's why you didn't let her tell us."

That was what I'd thought myself, but hearing Alexander say it was like dumping a bucket of cold water on my head, freezing the heated embarrassment into something else. It was one thing for me to doubt. It was quite another to know the five of them instantly jumped to my failure.

"You don't think there's any chance I can win this?"

Stone shook his head. "No. You're too sweet. They've got this wrong. They're sacrificing you. Why are you doing this, Sister Superior?"

"It has to be stopped." Gage shook his leg. "It's not too late."

I rose slowly. I shook with anger. "How dare the five of you doubt me? I am the Warrior." I'd never been so sure of anything. Any doubt I had fled in the face of this... betrayal. I hadn't told them, and I would own that guilt. This? It was something else entirely. "Maybe it's the five of you who can't handle this."

"You can't be the Warrior if you don't have five set guards. Sisters can't be sent down without five. If you're missing one, they'll have to replace one. They'll have to pick someone else. We were born to love you, Aspen, this is how we do it." Reed rose. "Sister Superior, I renounce my role. I choose not to be a guard. I will instead lead the guards. I'll be Brother Raven."

The area, which had been buzzing with whispers, fell silent. It was so quiet, my ears rang. Or maybe it was what Reed had just done. He renounced me? Tears flooded my eyes. I wasn't a crier, but I did right then. I couldn't have stopped myself if I wanted to.

"Reed?" What else was there to say? "Take it back."

He didn't look at me.

Sister Superior glared at him with the weight of a million daggers shooting from her eyes. I'd never seen her look like that before. "If that is your decision, it is your right to make it."

One of the elder Sisters rushed to her side, whispering something. What were they saying? I grabbed Reed's arm. This was the ultimate betrayal. My guard rejected me? Even though he'd stated his reasons, it didn't matter. A guard rejecting a Sister meant the guard rejected her soul. It was always the right. It just never happened.

My others were silent. Were they stunned or jumping ship, too? I couldn't even look at them. Yes, I'd kept a secret, but they'd all rejected me in some way. Reed wanted them to find me another guard. Should they find me five more?

"Sister? What happens now?" There I was, the so-called Warrior, the toughest Sister, weeping like a baby in front of the entire Sisterhood.

"The process has started."

Even as she spoke I could see it happening. Katrina was gone. Anne disappeared. The guards started popping away, some to watch as Ravens, some to be born into their guard roles. All of them leaving.

She walked toward me, standing right in front of me. "I'm afraid, child, that if your guards are rejecting you as they've all done, then you are not Sister material. I'm afraid we made a mistake. Someone else will have to defeat the Darkness. We won't have a Warrior."

I grabbed my neck. "No, Sister. Don't reject me. I can help in some way."

Her smile was small. "Indeed you can. You will be a wonderful human. The best of the best. But you won't be a Sister."

"Sister Superior," Reed and Alexander seemed to speak at the same time. "That was not the intention." It was Reed who spoke the last part.

"Be that as it may, it is done."

My body tingled. It burned. I was leaving. But something was wrong. I understood instantly. They were taking my powers, stripping me of them. The unwanted Sister. The one rejected. Warrior to nothing. My heart raced. No, this couldn't be happening. I screamed from the pain but also from the horror.

"No!" My guards were all shouting.

"We'll fix this. We didn't mean this. It was shocking. And Reed spoke too soon. It's not the way. No, Sister Superior. Aspen, we will fix this."

I understood two things right then from hearing the desperation in his voice, it was too late to do anything about this, and I'd never see them again. Humans didn't have guards. It was for the best. I sucked in my tears. They did nothing. I'd known it from the beginning. We weren't meant for each other. Not really. Sister Superior wasn't flawless. She'd made a mistake. I had no soul mates, which now made sense, since I wasn't a Sister anyway.

3

AFTER

I stepped away from the circle of their bodies, pulling my clothes out of Jamie's hands. I dressed without speaking. Other Sisters had lost their memories or some of them. They remembered their loves, their promises. They didn't remember all of it. Divinity had taken my powers and left me with total cognition of who I was supposed to be.

"Look, these powers are my problem to deal with. Not yours. I appreciate the five of you showing up, or being compelled to, or whatever. It's probably leftover from whatever was between us. But you can go. In fact, I'd like it if you did. There's a horse around here somewhere." I looked around. Where had my silver-gray rescuer gone? I hoped she was okay.

Gage lifted his eyebrows. "Bonney? Did she come to you? I brought her for Krystal."

I winced at the name. "You let the Healer get killed. For what? Some kind of guilt?"

My legs weren't great, but I made them move. I stepped away from them, walking out of the rain. I was still hot, but I wasn't their problem. I wouldn't let myself be. I held up my

26

hand. "Don't answer that. I don't want a recap. Okay? Krystal made a mistake. She shouldn't have given me these powers but now that she has, I'm going to at least use them appropriately. The Darkness is that way, leading a horde of demons and undead. I'm going to go try to kill him."

I didn't know how I was going to do that but as long as I was here and I had the power, I was going to go ahead and try. That was the best I could do.

"Right now?" Alexander stepped toward me. "You can hardly move."

I shook my head. "What I can and can't do is not your problem."

"I beg to differ, Sister. Everything about you concerns me. It always has."

I swallowed my anger. It wasn't going to get us anywhere. "The five of you rejected me. You doubted me. And yes, I lied. I did for months when I didn't tell you. As the speaker of divinity told me to. I apologize for that. This was all my fault. If you'd known who I was earlier you could have gotten yourselves out earlier and paired with a different Sister. So I apologize for all of it."

"Oh, enough with that," Stone yelled out a response. "You know we'd never have picked anyone else."

"Really?" I rounded on him. "You all jumped ship pretty quickly. Never mind this." I limped forward. "I reject the soul mating. See? I can do it, too. Be on your way. I'm busy."

"Well," Jamie laughed, "we reject your rejection."

I ignored him. They were right. I wasn't going to be ready to fight anyone tonight, but I could get there. I was stronger now than I'd been hours earlier. I slid down onto the ground by a tree. I'd wait until I was better. I'd get there. And then I'd figure out what to do.

Somehow.

Reed had been noticeably quiet. I looked around. Where

27

had he gone? As if I'd conjured him, he came through some other trees and walked toward us, holding a dead squirrel in his hands. He held it up. "If one of you will make a fire, I'm going to cook this for all of us."

"Good thinking." Gage strode toward him. "I'll make the fire."

Reed nodded. "Thanks."

I would have expected more hostility from them toward Reed. He'd blindsided them when he'd announced he'd be leaving the arrangement to be Brother Raven. Or maybe they were really all fine with it. I put my head on top of my knees. This was just... too much.

Jamie squatted down next to me. "You know how they say never to go to bed angry?"

I lifted my head. "Do they say that? Who says that?"

"It's one of those idioms people say."

I stopped to think if I'd ever heard that before. "Not any people I know, and I know people, having been a person myself for the last twenty-four years. Did you make that up?"

Jamie sighed. "I absolutely did not." When I would have answered, he took my hand in his, rubbing his finger over my knuckles. "I couldn't come near you for twenty-four years. Longer for me. But that's neither here nor there. It therefore stands to reason I would know different expressions than you know. My point is that it's not a good idea to go to bed angry, and we've had a lot of bedtimes without getting over our anger. Or..." He shook his head. "Your anger toward us. We're not angry with you. We all get it. If Sister Superior told me to keep something to myself I would as well. The question I still don't have an answer for is why did she do that." He squeezed my fingers. "Tonight, maybe you can go to bed not angry with us."

"I'm not angry. I'm tired." That was partially true. "Amazing that people have expressions right? Amazing they have anything at all. I mean, this is the end of days. Are people walking around making up sayings?"

He sat down fully next to me. "The end of existence doesn't seem to stop people from living their lives. They all know they can be possessed, yet they still leave the house every day. They have babies. They make plans. Maybe they do that because somewhere in their heads they know we will save them, that we will give them a future."

I snorted. "Maybe people are just dumb. Plain old dumb."

Just then my body grew cold, numbingly so. Heat gone, it was an abrupt, obvious pain, and I gasped. Jamie put his hand on my arm as realization dawned on me, coming in through the discomfort. That was a signal. A demon warning. I struggled to my feet. I was a Sister now. I would know when a true demon was around. And I had to do something about it. Even if my legs worked, I couldn't go around running from them anymore.

I'd never fought a demon outside of training. I'd rescued Sisters, spied on Katrina, broke into the Sisterhood, run for my life. I'd done it over and over again. But I'd never truly taken on a demon.

"Something is here." The bark of the tree bit into the part of my back still exposed. I'd really not dressed appropriately for having to suddenly become a Sister. "A demon."

Alexander looked left and right. "I don't see anything."

"Then I guess it's a good thing I can feel it."

He spoke again. "I'm not arguing with you that you can. I'm frustrated that I can't see it because if I can't see, we can't protect you. As a raven, I could see the demons. When they were around, my vision acted like they bathed the countryside in red."

"You're stuck with human eyes now, I guess." I limped forward. Being around a demon hadn't cured me of all my problems right off the bat. Apparently, I was going to have to figure out how to do this in pain and too injured to fully move.

I turned toward the trees. There hadn't been trees and then Krystal had brought them back. The trees would be safe for me, like a haven. That didn't mean that right on the other side there wasn't danger of the worst kind. I couldn't hide in the woods.

"Come out. Come out. Come out and play, *Sister*."

It taunted me. My spine stiffened. "Can you guys hear it?"

Reed nodded. "We can. It's speaking the common tongue, not an ancient language. That means it's been here a while. A strong one. Aspen, there is no harm in letting this one go."

He strode to me, his gait sure. In his hand was a piece of cooked squirrel. Or at least it wasn't fully raw. They'd hardly had enough time to really prepare the animal. "Open."

I did as he asked, and he placed it in my mouth. I didn't need instruction to chew. I bit down fast, eating the protein as the medicine I knew it to be. If I was going to fight, and despite his speech, Reed had to know I would, I had to have some food in my stomach. Even if it was only a small bite of squirrel.

"Stand back. If things go badly, get yourselves out of here." I wasn't prepared to be a Sister, but at least my powers came from within. They had nothing to help them be guards.

Alexander rolled his eyes. "Yeah, that's going to happen. We've all been waiting to protect you. I can promise you that we're not going to run while you fight."

"Even if we have to get sticks and stones." Gage ran a hand through his hair. "You do what you have to do. We're here."

I stepped away from them. On wobbly legs, I made my way toward the taunting demon. Humans ran from them if they had any foreknowledge they were there at all. I wasn't diminished anymore so even though my head screamed at me to flee as fast as I could, I walked toward it.

"So you're the new Sister." His voice sounded like a snake. His S sounds were elongated. Maybe it had to do with the fork in his tongue. I swallowed the bile rising from my stomach. This was the very first demon I'd ever conversed with.

Katrina had run a demonic sisterhood but at least the Sisters there had the chance to practice these things. This was going to be my live version, all alone with no one to direct me. I looked over my shoulder at Reed. "I don't suppose you have any advice, Brother Raven."

He winced. "I only dealt with the Sisters after they were changed. But you can do this. You did it very well in the other dimension. Or you can ignore it."

The longer I was in the presence of the demon, the clearer it was to me that I absolutely couldn't ignore it. My hands burned and my heart beat so loudly I could hear it in my ears. This was insanity. How did everyone live through this on a daily basis?

I'd spent years wanting it. I should have been appreciating not having to live with the pain.

Oh, who was I kidding? I loved this and that made me more than half sick in the head.

"You're the Sister who's supposed to kill us? That's just pathetic. That's..."

I didn't let it finish. I lifted my hands, and like I'd been doing this my whole life, I shot my powers through it. The world lost color. Where everything had been bright and painful, I could now only see in gentle black and white. The demon opened his mouth, but I couldn't hear him over the ringing in my ears. That was fine. I wanted him to shut up. I lifted my hand higher, the power burning my fingertips.

I pointed at his throat. The surge hit him there first. He melted, starting with his face, like I'd burned him from the inside out. Maybe I had done that. I was hot, on fire, and he was there. His skin went next, peeling off his body. His blood red eyes. I hadn't stopped to consider how much the thing looked like a lizard, but his tail went next.

I watched, as though from a distance, with almost no feeling inside of me. I'd been angry, scared, furious—but in the battle of this moment, I cared not that it happened. I hummed to myself. It was actually sort of interesting. Would I melt every demon I saw or just this one in particular? It pooled onto the ground in front of me. I cocked my head to the side as sound and light restored to my senses.

"Done." I turned to look at the guys who stood staring at me. Gage did, in fact, hold a rock in his hand. I guessed he really did intend to use it if needed. I stared at my hands, they shook. What was that about? "I..."

Stone was suddenly at my side, putting his hand on my arm. "You're okay. That was... amazing. I've never seen that before."

"That's because she's the Warrior." Pride laced his voice. "She was meant to be the strongest."

Nausea rolled through me. What had happened there? I hadn't felt... anything while I'd done that. Less than nothing. An absence of anything. "I think I might be sociopathic."

"What?" Jamie put his hands on his hips. "You're quite far from that. Katrina was sociopathic. You've always had the hugest heart of compassion."

Tears flooded my eyes. "Not when I was doing that. I felt nothing."

Reed stepped toward me. "Nothing at all?"

"Like all feeling disappeared." The world tilted left. Dizziness swept through me. Whatever I hadn't felt during the attack rushed at me now. The demon was gone but the fear remained. My hands shook even harder. "Something is wrong."

Reed tugged me against him. "It's all very new. Your body is adjusting. You're okay. Just breathe."

I tried. I really did. But the world went black.

◊◊◊

I WOKE UP FEELING WARM. SOMETHING SOFT WAS BENEATH me. A pleasant smell of food cooking wafted through the air. I wasn't wet anymore. I lifted my head as I wrenched open my eyes. Where was I? A small bedroom with yellow curtains greeted me. I'd never been in this place before. Sunlight streamed through the room. It looked like midday.

Next to me, someone stirred. It took me a second to recognize Gage. He murmured something but didn't wake. I brushed my finger against his cheek. Whiskers had grown in, blond on his pale skin, they were hard to see but rough on my fingers. He still didn't stir.

I'd been going through hell but so had the guys.

I snuck out of bed. The good news was my legs seemed to have decided to work. That was fantastic. Walking was a vital skill. I had a feeling I'd been lucky. The Darkness wasn't going to just melt for me. It was more like the universe gave me a trial run. Or something.

Maybe none of the powers that be were helping me at all. I was dressed in the same clothes I'd been in before, and they were stuck to my body. If this place, wherever we were, had a shower, I was going to try to use it and see about washing my clothes while I was at it. I hated being wet, but I detested damp clothes even more.

Amazing how two seconds in a house suddenly made me wimpy. Outside I always managed to pull myself together and handle whatever was thrown at me. Indoors? I turned so prissy I could hardly recognize myself.

Not that I knew many people.

My human family hadn't wanted that much to do with me. Even then, I'd pretty much lived between two worlds. I padded across the room and out the door in search of a bathroom. Gage didn't say anything so he either didn't wake or didn't mind my leaving. I looked over my shoulder. The first it was. He was really, really out of it.

Voices carried down the hall. I followed them to the source.

"You're lucky the five of us aren't throwing you out the window and I'm including Aspen in that. She should want you tossed, too. You did this to us. Now you want to give orders? I've got news for you, Reed, you're not One anymore."

Alexander's angry tone was the first I could clearly make out as I quietly approached.

Reed snorted. They were in a kitchen, and I could see him leaning against a counter through the partially open doorway. "As if you could throw me out a window. And I'm Aspen's One. Get over yourself. I didn't cause this. Sister Superior and her pompous know it all bullshit when she only half understands the universe did by making Aspen lie to us. I tried to save her. I've lived in hell ever since. You want to make this about me? Fine. Do so. The only person I'll give my apology to is Aspen. She deserves it. I blew it. But the rest of you? You didn't have to abandon ship."

So things were not as hunky dory as they were pretending earlier. They were pulling it together for me. Sadness swept through me. No one had been closer than the five of them, and I hated thinking of Reed on the outside. He'd been the glue to hold everyone together.

Before entering the room, I cleared my throat to stop them from talking. Alexander's eyes widened. "You're up. Where is Gage?"

"Out cold." I pointed at Jamie's glass. "Tell me there is something warm in there."

His grin came fast. "There is, indeed. Here, I'll get you some coffee. We arrived in time to see the owner of this house fleeing for her life. The hordes of dead are scaring people away. We told her you were a Sister and she offered us the house for our use, food included. It's been so long since I have eaten anything. I haven't needed to as a raven. I didn't feel any hunger. Did any of you?"

The three of them shook their heads. That was so weird. I'd not stopped to think about that at all. They were never hungry? Not even in the way birds were? "How is it eating now?"

He grinned broader. "She had pie. This is a rich person's house. What do people in this area do to earn? Are there nobles this far out?"

"I don't know where we are to answer that."

Reed sighed. "This is the house of a mid-level noble. They are still ranchers here, and this far from the Deadlands they are still able to survive without having to destroy the peasants too badly. You're forty five minutes by foot from home, Aspen."

"Oh." I swung around. "I actually know this place. I passed here many times." The yellow curtains tipped me off. I could see them from the street because the windows were often open. "There's a huge lake nearby. We're not far from the train station."

Gage nodded. "Right. We need to get on one of those trains. We think the best thing to do is get you to Anne. She'll know how to help you if anyone will."

I supposed that made sense, except for one giant problem. "Can we just abandon these people? The horde is here."

Alexander answered. "What we know is that the final battle will come with Anne involved. That tells us you have to

35

be with her. I hate to leave them unprotected, too. We'll come back when it's over. We'll come back and help."

Reed shook his head. "Truth? People need help everywhere. This place is not unique nor more deserving because you happened to grow up here." He held up his hand. "I know. That's a terrible thing to say. Sometimes truth hurts. You don't need platitudes."

He was right. I'd never had time for nonsense. Still, he could take his holier than thou and shove it where the sun didn't shine. "I don't need sweet words but you're taking your bad mood out on me. Not okay, either."

Reed winced. He wasn't the only one who dealt in truth. Gage ran into the room, his eyes wild. "Fuck. Okay. You're okay."

Jamie rolled his eyes. "Language. We're in the presence of our Sister."

I laughed. "Your Sister has heard that word before. I'm okay, Gage. I just didn't want to wake you up. I grew up with humans, guys. I've heard that and a lot worse. My mother was a psycho who occasionally tortured people in the basement. She wasn't even possessed. I guess when you're not good enough to be a Sister you don't get the pick of the litter in human parents."

They were all silent and not in a comfortable way. Maybe the less said about my upbringing the better if I wanted to keep things on the pleasant side. "We don't need to do this, okay? We can separate. I'd appreciate the help getting to Anne's. After that, if you've just had enough..."

Stone set down his drink with a loud clunk just as Jamie handed me one. "We're not going to have had enough. Stop trying to get rid of us. We need to repair this. And I don't know that we're ever going to see eye-to-eye on what happened and who should have done what. By divinity, there were times I wanted to kill Reed and not just for his role but for his absence in the planning. No one sees angles like he does. We were all meant to be together. End of story. Do you think it's possible you could forgive us and move on? Right now. Right here."

That was a good question. Could I just decide to stop the feelings I'd held for over two decades? Right here in this stranger's kitchen? "If I am going to make that happen, I need the fighting to stop from all of you. You have to do it, too. Whatever your issues are with Reed"—I looked at him as I spoke—"whatever your issues are with them, it stops now. We all have to agree that we'll never come to consensus and maybe we don't have to, but we can work together on this task." I shook my head. "I don't think I can throw myself back into the whole 'we're all in love' thing. I can do the getting over the anger. I can make that happen. Truth is it's draining, and if last night showed me anything, it was that I need all my energy for what is happening. I... I missed you guys. Forgiveness I can decide to do and make that happen. Love is another thing all together."

Alexander nodded. "Fine. That's not unreasonable. But you will love us again. I know you will. There isn't a future where we're not together. There never was one. From the second we spotted you with the Sisters, all five of us knew you were ours. There wasn't even discussion, there was clarity."

When he spoke of memories like that one, it was hard not to believe him. They needed to understand. "I've been living pretty much alone since it was safe for me to do so. I'm not the same woman you saw on the fighting field."

"It wasn't on the fighting field we saw you," Reed's voice was low. "It was by the purple lake. You did look alone. And we knew that without you all five of us were alone in a crowd. We know your loneliness, too. I've been helping Sisters find their guards endlessly for what feels like forever. I watched it work, and I watched it not work. The spark that lit or didn't. I've manipulated fates to bring others together, the whole time knowing that my own love would always be out of my grasp. If you came somewhere, I was instantly pulled away. I couldn't even catch a glimpse of you. I didn't know for sure the four of them were even down here. I get the impression it has been the same for them. I know lonely. Let's not stay that way anymore. Let's believe in the future."

"Believe in the future in the end of days. What a terribly difficult concept." I walked to the window. "Okay. I'm willing to try." Still, I couldn't look at any of them. "Tell me there's a shower in this place."

❧ 4 ❧

We walked together toward the train station. I'd determinedly done this trip myself a bunch of times. I'd get news through the gossip grapevine in whorehouses or pubs about things going wrong with the Sisterhood. I'd rush there and intervene. Katrina never gave regular humans any thought. I'd been able to get in and out of there many times—saving Krystal twice—alone. I'd felt like I was doing something to assist people who had once been my comrades in battle.

Now I would join them again. Would they want to see me? Or would they know I didn't really belong with them?

My body was stiff. The shower had helped me get clean and relaxed but now walking around again without any rest had left me aching. It didn't matter. I'd never cared about my personal pain. We eventually made it there. I stared at the empty tracks, lost in my own thoughts, and the guys seemed to be, too.

None of us had spoken. For the first time in a long time, I wasn't hungry. Gage had collected all the food from the house and put it in backpacks that he and Stone had also lifted from the residence. We were taking the owner's offer of use of the house literally; we were even taking things with us. Hopefully, no one minded.

"Did we actually pack up some of their clothes?"

Reed shrugged. "Better that than be stuck with one pair each and nothing to do if they get wrecked. Plus, you're going to be saving everyone on the planet. I think they can all temporarily donate to the cause."

I shook my head as amusement flooded me. Not one of them had ever been human. "I don't know that they'll see it that way, but we'll go with that for now."

The train sounded in the distance. There had been more problems with these trains than I cared to count. They derailed, had demon attacks, stopped moving randomly, and half the time they didn't get where they were going. But we were going to go with the idea that I'd get to Anne's somehow. This was the first step.

Skepticism had been my savior for a long time. I wasn't prepared to believe I'd board this train and take it all the way to Anne's without a problem. That wasn't how this worked for me. Nothing was simple. Still, I paid for our tickets— since the guys had no money—and boarded. That would pretty much be the end of my money. I was going to have to find a job and earn some more unless the Sisterhood wanted to fund me. They had benefactors who helped them, but I'd never been on the receiving end of it and wouldn't be until I got there.

The food in the backpacks would have to feed us until we arrived. We couldn't buy anything.

Others made their way to rooms that would act like cabins on their trip. We piled into uncomfortable seats that would have to suffice for the days and nights we traveled. I'd seen Sisters and their guards on trips before. They'd never known who I was, but I'd stared incessantly at them. They'd been in luxury.

Regret filled me that I couldn't do the same for mine. A muscle ticked in my jaw. Nothing was ever easy.

"You okay?" Alexander looked almost too big for the seat. It was going to be a long couple of days for him.

I tried not to wince at how obviously transparent I was. "I feel badly that I can't treat us to better rooms. On my own, I never noticed it. But all of you sitting here for days? I am acutely aware that you have been stuck on the wrong end of the Sister stick again."

"You know," Stone answered instead of Alexander. "Most Sisters wouldn't give that a second thought. Our comfort? They take the bed and the guards sleep on the floor outside the room. I'd rather sit here in chairs with you and have you thinking about things like that than any other Sister in any time."

The others nodded as though they agreed. Still, as the train pulled out to travel across the countryside, I didn't feel better about it. Stone's words banged around in my head. A lot of time passed before I could find my words again. "What you said was funny."

Stone opened his eyes. I hadn't realized he'd been resting. All of them but Reed lay back with their eyes closed. They must have had some unspoken decision to take turns. The others didn't budge, but Stone regarded me quietly, as though he didn't mind that I'd woken him.

"What part was funny, my heart?" Heat flared in his gaze when he spoke, moving through me until I wanted to squirm from it.

I made myself stay still. I couldn't be that affected just from his speaking to me, could I?

I cleared my throat. "In any time. Some of the Sisters

aren't here now. The ones I was with. They were here hundreds of years ago. Katrina was here long before me."

He nodded. "Time is different, here versus there. I could be visiting there for a minute and find hours or days passed here. You were all sent to whenever you were supposed to be sent and your guards to the same place and time. Or that was the idea. Plans went askew."

Reed shifted in his chair. "I tried to help with that. I got people to a place where they could at least meet. Helped stir memories, that kind of thing."

"Time is... fluid then. For us. Not for humans. Hard to think of myself as not human but there you go. I... It just feels funny, that's all."

"Why?" Stone took my hand, lacing our fingers together. "What's funny about it?"

"I've never understood certain aspects of our lives." I threw my free hand in the air. "Maybe it's above my level."

He might have asked me more, but the train made a groaning sound, and I jumped, landing between Stone and Reed in an awkward position where the edge of the armrest between them jammed into my rear.

"Hey." Reed pulled me fully onto his lap. "It's okay."

I shook a little bit in his arms. "I hate these trains. I do this all the time. But they derail, they get toppled. I don't want to be trampled to death. Give me a demon any day. That wasn't as bad as this."

He rubbed my back gently, eventually pressing his forehead to it. "I don't think I've ever seen you afraid before."

Was he kidding? "I'm scared all the time. Both now and in the other world. All. The. Time."

"Then you're really good at hiding it." He continued to rub my back. "I get scared, too. Mostly when I think about somehow losing you. Failing you. Never getting to say I'm sorry. I am sorry, Aspen. I didn't mean for this to happen. I freaked out. All I could think was keeping you from vanishing if you lost. I... I didn't consider the ramifications. I didn't know what would happen. This is all on me."

Stone looked away, quickly, as though he wanted to give us a minute of privacy in a completely un-private situation. Next to us, Alexander started to snore lightly. They really had to have been out of it to have missed my shriek.

"I appreciate your apology. I know you always have the best intentions, Reed. Sometimes it was hard to live with it but... okay, we agreed to move forward. That means I give you the benefit of the doubt on this. I forgive you." That hadn't been at all hard to say. "I'll move, sorry."

Reed shook his head. "No, don't. I like you here on my lap."

Stone stretched out his legs in front of him, closing his eyes again. "See you both in a couple of hours. I'm up next."

Now, I felt badly that I'd woken him. He took my feet in his hands, drawing them to him and placing them on his lap. He patted them once before he leaned his neck in what had to be an uncomfortable angle and closed his eyes.

I sighed. "These chairs suck."

Reed laughed, low in his throat. "I don't know. I kind of like them right now." He kissed the side of my neck. "Remember when we wondered if it would be better to touch each other in human bodies? This is my first time in one. As a raven, I didn't have all these sensations. Fuck, do I now."

My cheeks warmed. I wasn't unaware of the reaction he was having, his body hardened beneath me. It made me hot inside, but I resisted the urge to squirm. His light kiss on my skin threw me off as well. He was right. Human bodies really felt things. I had for twenty-four years but nothing like this. This was something else.

I sucked in my breath. "Reed, we're in chairs in the middle of the train. I don't think this is the time."

"I'm going to keep my hands to myself. I promise. Just wanted to touch you for a second. To remind myself you're real and not a figment of my imagination. Lean back on me, I'll keep you safe. The train isn't going to do anything bad. I promise."

I didn't point out that he wasn't capable of making that kind of promise. Not in the least. But he was comfortable and didn't seem bothered by me on his lap. I was tiny, and Reed was big. I didn't need to worry about being too large for him, even in these horrible chairs.

I leaned back. The train made a regular swoosh noise and even the jolts that normally left me tense the entire trip didn't sound so bad because there was the sound of Reed's heartbeat to accompany them.

I jolted awake sometime later. I hadn't been dreaming, and it took me a moment to realize why I was awake. Reed was still beneath me, his breathing even. He slept. Next to me, Stone was awake. He sat up, staring at me as though he wanted to know what the issue was. The second I realized it, he did too. We must already be connected that way.

My powers were on. They hurt. The world changed, my vision clouding before it changed to black and white. I groaned. I guessed that wasn't going to be a one-time thing then. I was going to see this way when the demons were around.

"Guys." Stone rose, taking my hand and drawing me up with him. The others awoke. "She's on."

Gage looked over his shoulder and then around. "Aspen? Point us in the direction."

"Can I just say how disconcerting it is to see this way? Black and white?"

Reed shook his head. "I've never heard this before. It's unique to you, love. Didn't happen in the other dimension?"

Everything had been shockingly bright and clear there. I

shook my head no. "I don't know where the demon is. I'm going to have to go look for it. But it must be close enough to have turned me on, so to speak."

Reed pointed in front of him. "Jamie, you're with me. Alexander behind her. Nothing comes from behind. Gage and Stone left and right."

This was the moment. Would they listen to Reed or were they going to challenge his authority? I shouldn't be worrying about this; I should just trust them to handle their own business. Yet, I couldn't move until I knew. There was too much on the line here.

Alexander nodded, and it was like I could breathe. Okay, this was going to work. He winked at me before he stepped back so I could cross in front of him. Did he know? It was time to manage the demon problem. I didn't want to look at the world with these dead eyes anymore. I wanted my color back.

My hands buzzed. Maybe it was because I wasn't wet and injured but my powers didn't hurt nearly as badly this time. They were just on and they weren't going to turn off until I did something with them. Choice clearly played no role in this life.

Somewhere in the back of my head, I heard a baby crying. I stopped moving. That wasn't a sound present, more like something I was hearing because my powers were on. Where was the baby? Was I just making all of this up?

"Jamie, can you hear a baby crying?"

He paused, tilting his head to the side. "No. You hear that?"

"I do." And I could even tell which direction it came from now. I pointed toward the back of the train. "That way."

I marched forward. None of them tried to hinder me but rather they hurried, staying in their positions as best they could, considering the unusual maneuvering we had to do on the train. The sound of the baby banged around in my head. This had to be the right way. A thought dawned on me, and I stopped my charge forward but only so I could look outside.

Sisters always saw the ravens. That was part of the deal. I was a Sister now. Shouldn't they be up there observing this mess I was in down here? Didn't seeing them up there indicate we were on the right journey?

I scooted past an unknowing human to look out a window. Sure enough, a huge grouping of the birds flapped their wings to keep up with the train.

"Guess someone took over for you, Reed," Gage spoke low so others wouldn't hear us. "Any idea who they are?"

My One searched the skies next to me. "No. They all look like birds to me now. They were somehow still men before. Any number of them could have taken the role. I really don't know."

Six of them were ahead of the others, one out in front. The cries of the baby increased. It was time for me to do whatever this was. I turned toward my guys. "I don't even know what to tell you to do because I don't know what's going to happen now."

"We're here. Still without weapons," Alexander spoke through clenched teeth. "But we're here."

The sound of the crying eventually led me to a room. The kind I'd envying others for having. Should I knock on the door? I chewed on my lip as I considered this. Was a demon going to invite me inside?

I tried the handle and it turned. Knowing I could be walking in on any number of things that were none of my business, I stepped into the room. Better to apologize than not get what I needed.

At first I saw no one. Was the room empty? Then the truth dawned on me. There were two people on the bed, both dead. I stormed farther in to get a better look. There was a crib in the corner and next to it was a demon pulling the life out of a baby. A tiny human who no longer had any parents. Anger surged through me.

The demon resembled a human. I bet it could walk around if it wanted and not be noted by those who couldn't see the horns on its head the way I could.

"Sister?" Jamie called my attention. "What do you see?"

"A dead demon." Or at least it would be.

I lifted my hand as it jumped to its feet. It spit venom at me, and I darted out of the way. Oh, so it was one of those gross beings. I didn't know what they were called. I'd missed my training down here, but I knew enough to get out of the way.

"Stay back," I called out to my guys. I didn't want them getting hurt. His venom would scald whatever skin it came in contact with. It might destroy their clothes.

"We can't see it, Aspen," Reed answered my instructions.

"Then even more reason to get in the doorway and not move."

The demon opened his mouth and called out to me in a language I didn't speak. That was okay. I didn't have to understand him to kill him. I lifted my hand and my power flew at him. He wasn't as easy as the first demon I'd killed. No, this one knew how to defend himself. He spit more venom and rushed at me.

The guys couldn't see him, but he was perfectly solid to me. We struck the floor hard. My back immediately ached, but I had no time to worry about pain. I was a fighter and damned if I didn't suddenly remember how.

"Aspen," Gage yelled out my name. I wanted to reassure him but there was no time.

I struck upward. The power in my hands made them sharp. I had the demon by the throat. But we both knew this wasn't going to be won in the physical plain. He needed me to stay solid and that was just what I didn't want to do. I dug deep inside of myself, letting free the power that my cells were still trying to incorporate.

I gasped as the pain became pleasure a second before the demon and I floated into nothingness together. Damn, but this felt good. I didn't have time to revel in my now fully working powers. No, I had to kill this evil from the world before he could hurt anyone else. We were nothing but atoms, and I was going to turn him into nothing at all.

I didn't know how long we raged with each other but one long burst of light from me and he was no more. One second he was there and the next he was gone. For a second, I floated in the ether, I could stay like this if I wanted to. The thought struck me as sad, and I pushed it away. There were things waiting for me. People who wanted to reclaim something we'd lost. We weren't perfect. I might never completely get over what happened. But I could let it go and have a future—for however long it lasted.

The Darkness might consume me. If the venomous demon had gotten his way, I would have been destroyed to nothingness. I finally understood what the end might mean for me, why I might vanish. If I lost, I'd be the demon I just ended. I'd be... gone.

That was my gift or my curse. I could end existence, leaving no footprint of the demon behind. But they could do that to me, too.

That was the fate of the Warrior.

One way or another.

I rushed back into my body, reappearing on the ground where I'd been. Light returned first, the black and white not fading to color. I blinked. Why wasn't the color back?

Five faces came into my view, all of them staring down at me. A second later, Reed lifted me from the ground to a standing position while Alexander supported my back. All of them had their hands on me in some way, Jamie's on my cheek.

Gage kissed the top of my head. "You vanished."

"That is what they do." A muscle ticked in Reed's cheek. "But watching others do it is not the same as watching you. I think I aged ten years. You clearly did it. Demon's gone."

"Demon is gone, yes. I still can't see color."

Just then the train jolted to a stop, and we all went flying backward. With the force of the collision, I went into the baby's crib, grabbing the small boy as he flew out of it. He landed on my chest, a small cry escaping him. I stared down at him. I used to take care of some of the neighborhood children to earn gold for the trips to help the Sisters. I didn't think I'd ever taken care of one this little but he seemed okay.

I managed to scramble from the floor, baby in my arms. The guys followed me to their feet.

"What happened? And whatever it is I'd like to point out that I hate these trains and clearly have good reason to."

Reed shook his head. "I am constantly breaking promises to you. I'm not making any more."

I tapped him on the arm. "You said I wouldn't get hurt. I didn't. And the train is intact. Just stopped. Can someone take the baby? I think there must still be a demon somewhere."

Gage stepped forward. "I'll take him."

I handed him the baby.

"The name says James on his embroidered blanket. I'm going to go find him a human. If there are still demons around, he needs to be safe and we need you to concentrate on that. Good job basically saving his life in the crash."

They hadn't seen the demon sucking James' life. That was probably a good thing. They didn't need that imagery.

Outside, people were screaming, and the sound drifted to me. I steeled my shoulders. My battles weren't done yet.

I rushed out of the room, four of my guys on my heels, with Gage presumably staying back to find a human for the baby. I trusted him to find a good one. There were too many people who would harm a child, or give them to demons. That little one had just lost his parents. I'd mourn for his loss later, when I wasn't seeing the world in black and white with another crisis to handle immediately.

Or at least I hoped I would. It was hard to feel much of anything while the world looked this wrong—as though I had a black and white veil between myself and reality.

The passengers were in chaos, and I darted around people who frantically fought to escape the train. I followed one through an opened exit and jumped down to see what was happening. Hordes of people chanted in a circle, holding hands. They blocked the train tracks, swaying back and forth as though they heard music. I stopped and stared because as odd as that scene was—and it at least made sense why the conductor had so abruptly stopped the train from progressing —the live chanters weren't what startled me.

It was who—or rather what—was in the center of the circle. The largest demon I'd ever laid eyes on stood with his hands to the sky, seeming to draw energy from the crowd. He looked like a cross between a giant troll and a horse. It was an odd combination.

I stared at him for a second before I grabbed Alexander's arm. "Are they worshiping him? Can you see what I see?"

He nodded. "They sure seemed to be. Willingly. They don't seem to be enthralled."

I agreed. Their eyes were clear. They weren't moving like the way a possessed human would. "Then why are they doing this?"

"They're worshiping the demon. That's all I can say...

they're deliberately feeding it with their own energy... they want to be doing this."

Next to me Jamie sighed. "Makes you wonder sometimes if humanity is worth saving, right?"

I placed my hand on his arm. "We all have those thoughts. Trust me. But this is our job. I guess I have to get to it. Through them."

"That's why you have us." Stone touched the back of my neck. "To kick the ass of any of them that try to get near you."

I shouldn't have been smiling, except I was, because life was sometimes perversely amusing.

❧ 5 ❧

I stepped toward the scene. I didn't know whether it was the baby who woke me or this impending mess, but I had to get these fools away from the train tracks and the demon in the center of it gone. Maybe all of this was great practice for the Darkness. Maybe I just had bad luck. Or this was the world we lived in. I didn't have to overthink it. I just had to deal with the mess.

I looked up at the sky. The ravens circled, watching. What were they doing? I'd have to ask Reed. I meant, really, what was the point?

I had to do this whether they approved of it or not. I shook my head. I wanted my vision back. Who knew I should have been appreciating color while I could? I sighed.

"Everybody move." I pushed through the linked-arm crowd, having to break one of the links as I walked toward the demon.

He turned to stare at me. "A Sister? What are you doing here? Shouldn't you be holed up, fretting over things?"

The demon laughed at its bad joke. The crowd giggled. Was he some sort of demonic performance artist? I guessed he hadn't heard of me. The other two had seemed to know who or what they were dealing with when I'd arrived.

Was there not some demon communication where they all knew the same things? I needed to be caught up fast on my demonic schooling. But first, I had to get through this.

"Why do you do it?" I called out to him, approaching slowly. My hands burned with wanting to take him down, but he was huge, and I had to be careful. "Why are you here spending time acting like some kind of sideshow act?"

He laughed again, which made the crowd laugh. That was going to get on my last nerve very quickly. "Haven't you been paying attention? The Darkness brought us all here. This is our world now. You can join us. I'd love another follower." He extended his hand as though I was supposed to take it. I stared at it for a long second.

"I have been paying attention. Deeply. And you just reminded me why I'm going through all of this. The Darkness brought you here."

I plowed into him with everything I had. We didn't have to vanish together; this didn't need to take place at the cellular level. He was big, and he might be able to trick these foolish humans into worshiping him, but that didn't fool me. His size had put me off. I should have realized it made him bulky.

I gritted my teeth. Tiredness weighed on me. I wasn't going to let it defeat me. Taking down the demon took no time. He exploded in pieces, some of it spraying on me like gook. I gagged. Wearing his insides hadn't been something I ever needed to do.

Color rushed back fast. I realized that I panted. I'd not even realized when I started doing it. I put my hand on my hips and doubled over. Panic overtook me. There was nothing worse than not being able to catch my breath. Okay, maybe there were worse things. But that was all I could focus on right then.

"Get her," one of the humans called. Get me? Great. I wasn't in any condition to...

"You aren't getting anywhere near her." The guys had surrounded me. It was Gage who had spoken. "Take one step toward her and you are all dead."

I guessed they didn't listen. The humans rushed toward us, men and women, all of different ages, their hands in front of them like claws. I had to catch my breath. There were at least fifty of them, and I had five guys.

I didn't know if they were going to be able to take on ten people each. I had to help. I needed to...

The ravens dove toward the ground. That seemed sort of odd. Reed must have thought so too because his mouth fell open. I guessed under his command the ravens didn't come and participate in fights. That seemed to be against the rules as far as I could remember them. Before they were guards, ravens had to be pretty hands off unless directed by Brother Raven.

The six who landed shifted quickly to their human form, and for a second, I wondered if I'd lost my mind. Krystal turned to me, taking my hand. "You've done enough. Let us help you. This is not going to end you. Not if I can help it."

"You're a bird." I sounded ridiculous, but this was beyond even what I could imagine. "And you died."

She stroked my hair once. "Sweet friend, it is so complicated. For now, let's just say that I am the queen of reincarnation. They seem to like to bring me back. There are ten of the guards now. Just breathe with me." She touched the side of my face. "Oh, no, you're going to faint."

And just like that, I did.

My head throbbed like someone had beat a stick into my forehead over and over. I groaned, and a hand touched my cheek. "You're okay."

Jamie's voice was soothing. He said I was okay, I believed him. He must have lain next to me; his breath was on my cheek a second before he pressed a kiss to it. I sighed. Affection really did help. I'd always heard that, just had little cause to experience it. He kissed me again.

Sounds started to trickle into my consciousness. The train must be moving. We swayed, and the engine noises permeated the fog around my head.

"Just rest, beautiful. Krystal says you used way too much power for so early in your attack. You need sleep. Close your eyes. You're not alone. You won't be alone a second. I promise you that."

I hadn't really been able to open my lids, but I gave up trying to be aware of anything. I drifted off again. When I came back to myself, my head hurt less. My eyes obeyed, opening on command, and my stomach grumbled. I was hungry.

I looked around the room. Where was I? I didn't recognize the cabin, and we hadn't been able to afford anything. How were we in one?

I leaned back on my elbows to get a better glance.

"You're up." Jamie was still there. He yawned, rolling toward me. He must have been asleep next to me on the bed. "Good morning. You slept twenty-four hours. We would have worried, but Krystal is reassuring."

That was right. Krystal. My gorgeous, blonde friend had saved the planet with her healing skills, died when she gave me her powers, and was somehow back as a raven. None of it made any sense. "How?"

"It's a long story. Sounds like divinity made her Brother, or rather Sister, Raven. They're here with us right now. Actually, in the other room. They have money. An endless supply, it seems. I haven't asked them how. I don't want to know. But when the train took off again we had rooms. Five connected. Half the passengers had disappeared anyway and you saved that baby. The conductor was happy to help us."

Krystal had managed to do what I hadn't which was make everyone comfortable. I'd have to thank her as soon as I could move. Jamie leaned over and kissed me. I closed my eyes and didn't fight it. I wanted this. He was so sweet, always had been, and I wanted to be lying in this bed with him kissing more than I did anything else in the world.

He didn't make moves to do anything but kiss. I wanted more. But this was Jamie and he'd never been aggressive even before things fell apart. I pulled him closer. "All of you."

He moaned against me, his movements becoming more dominant. I loved it. I let him lead, happily following where he went. He took his mouth from mine, kissing down my neck. I ran my hand through his black hair. He was so much bigger than me, and yet he never made me feel small. Cherished was the word I'd use for how Jamie treated me. How had I forgotten how this felt? Why hadn't I dived right back into it?

Fear. I'd been letting it dominate everything, even when I was brave, I was afraid. No more. I wanted Jamie. I was going to have this love for as long as I could, and I wasn't going to hold back from it because the past wrecked my life. There was a future, even if it was short, and I was going to hold onto it.

Starting right this second.

He pulled at my shirt, and I took it off. Jamie stared down at my breasts, his eyes wide. "You're so beautiful."

I grabbed his chin before I lifted up to kiss him. "So are you. Take your shirt off so we can be in this together. I think that's the point. I've never done this before."

His cheeks reddened. Jamie was the one of my five to really wear his emotions on his sleeve. Whatever he felt, he demonstrated on the outside. "I wondered. I... I know I don't have the right to question what you were doing. We lost that. But I always hoped it would just be us and you."

"People have lots of reasons for intimacy. And sometimes they have lots of reasons for not being that way. For me, I think I hoped for the impossible, that someday we'd be just like this. I waited."

He tugged off his shirt. Jamie was built like I remembered him, solid as a rock. His muscles had muscles. I ran my hand over his chest to feel the definition of them, and he trembled beneath my fingertips.

"I can really feel things here, acutely. Your fingertips on my skin, it's like butterfly wings."

He had always been a poet. I kissed him, drawing him back to me, and he kissed me for a while. Then he scooted down, kissing his way to my breasts. They were small, the right size for my frame, and I'd never thought much about them. They tingled a second before Jamie took my left nipple in his mouth. He moaned, his hips jerking against me when he did. He reached out with his hand and massaged the other one while he tugged and sucked on my nipple.

I closed my eyes. This was... wow. His hips jerked again and this time my own body rose against him. I cried out, anticipation and my body heating up at the same time urged me forward. I opened my lids to stare at the beauty that was Jamie.

He let go of one nipple and changed to the other. His eyes were glazed; he was seriously focused on his task, and I loved it. He could have me any way he wanted me, for as long as he did. I'd never been so anticipatory and satisfied at the same time. There would never be another first moment like this for either of us.

We eventually got each other's clothing off. We were arms and legs, banging into each other as we went. At some point I even elbowed him in the chin. He laughed and rubbed it. Jamie had the brightest smile. He could light up the universe with it. How could there be evil in the world when there were passionate embraces and adoration from good souls like Jamie?

I didn't dwell on that question. It came and went. I didn't have to worry about anything, not when I was here with him. He scooted down again, his legs now hanging off the bed. He touched my core almost reverently, raising his gaze to meet my own.

"You sure?"

I nodded. "I... I love you Jamie. I always have. I'm sorry that I held us back from this. I'm sorry I held off in this crazy world. If I'd admitted that I never stopped, never could have. I..."

He practically jumped back on top of me, catching himself with his elbows. He kissed me again and again and again. I reached between us and stroked his cock in my hand. It grew even larger as I caressed him. He moaned against my mouth.

I loved how he reacted. I adored that I could have this effect on him. He lifted up enough to press a finger inside of me.

"You're so warm. I can't..."

"Jamie." I kissed his shoulder before I bit down on it, slightly. "Come inside of me."

He nodded, his face serious. "Next time I want to play for a long time."

I was hardly going to argue. "We'll be together like this again. And again."

He bit down on my lower lip once before he moved just enough to put himself in place. Neither of us had done this before. It took a minute to get things exactly right but before long he pushed inside of me. I cried out.

"You okay?" He pressed his forehead to mine.

I nodded slowly. "It's so different than anything I've done before. Jamie, you're deep inside of me."

Inch-by-inch my body welcomed him inside. I'd never shared this part of myself and yet it felt the most natural thing to do. We found our rhythm. He'd press in and pull out, my hips greeting him with every pass. His long, hard cock rubbed my clit each time. I panted for him. The jolts carried me through pleasure.

Jamie lifted my leg to get a deeper thrust and soon we were both calling out our climaxes. I pushed over the edge, crying out into the universe as my orgasm rocked me in a way nothing else ever had. He followed me, calling out my name as though it were a prayer while he emptied inside of me.

He never collapsed, keeping his weight off me until he could roll us over, my tinier frame on top of his. Jamie joined our lips one last time. "I love you. To me, you have always been eternity. Divinity. All that is right in the universe. The point of anything at all."

My consciousness shifted. One second I stared at his lovely face, and the next I saw a scene somewhere else.

"Jamie." Reed's voice caught my attention, but I refused to turn away from where I stood. My best friend appeared next to me. I understood immediately that I wasn't me in this moment, I was Jamie. I was seeing something from Jamie's eyes.

What was happening?

"It's hard not to watch her all day, I know." Reed stared out in the distance.

There I was. It took me a minute to recognize myself. I didn't really look like he saw me. The essentials were the same, I supposed. My hair was long and black, shiny. But I'd never, not even in the other existence, shown with light the way he saw me. My cheekbones weren't quite so high, my smile not so bright. My clothes never moved flawlessly with me.

Where was this that he watched me? I was on a field, stepping next to Teagan. She said something, and I nodded my head. It was at some point during our training. I didn't remember, particularly.

"I still can't believe Sister Superior said she could be ours. If she agrees." I bit down on my fingernail. "Do you think she will? We can make ourselves more worthy. I know we can."

"We can and we will, my brother." Reed touched my arm. "We'll take care of her. We'll see her fulfill her destiny and be at her side."

I nodded. "We will."

That was a certainty.

I was ripped back into my body with a jolt. What was that? I gasped. Jamie grinned at me, a huge smile taking up most of his face. But it was his eyes that caught my attention. They had gone white. They were fully that way, like Sisters. Did mine even look that white yet?

"What did I do to you?" The shaking of my voice matched the terror in my soul. I'd hurt him. Something had gone wrong? "We'll get help."

"No," he took my hand and kissed it, "my love. All of Krystal's guards have white eyes. It's called co-joining. It's a meeting of souls. I'll be better able to help you with your powers now. We want this. All five of us. More than anything. Relax and feel it. Can you? I am in your mind, you are in mine."

I tried to breathe through my utter terror. He was right. There in the back of my consciousness was something that hadn't been there before. A presence. It took a second to recognize, but now I could feel the essential sweet strength that was Jamie. More than that, his love for me was there for me to feel completely. The sheer power of it brought tears to my eyes.

"You." It was hard for me to speak, so I had to say it twice. "You love me."

He nodded slowly. "I do so much that I can't breathe for needing you. I love you, and I can feel how you love me, too, Aspen. Forever. This is eternity. Do you see what I mean?"

I did. I kissed him. This man who held my soul as tightly as I held his.

I FOUND EVERYONE ELSE IN A KITCHEN. THE SMELL OF FOOD wafted to my nose. Who was cooking? It was one of Krystal's guards, Paden, who stood at the stove cooking eggs. The trains had private kitchens? It was like a different world.

Krystal pulled me into a hug. She smelled sweet, like sugar. "You're okay and, yep, just as I thought, your eyes are white. You're one of us now."

"I still can't believe you're not dead. You gave me your powers."

She let me go with a squeeze. "I have new powers. We're still in this fight together. All I did was give you what you needed. What we needed you to have."

Had my guys told her the truth? "Krystal, I think you need to know some of the facts of this..."

She interrupted me with a wave of her hand. "Don't fret about manipulation. Alexander filled me in. This was always a path and no one out maneuvers Beelzebub. Not even the Darkness himself. I'd say things worked out just fine. We have a chance now. Thanks to you. Oh, that's terrible. Too much pressure. Come eat."

I was tugged into a hug from behind. The strong arms had

to be Stone. As I turned slightly, I was glad to see I was right. I needed to be able to tell them apart by touch alone. It seemed to be one of those things I should be able to do.

"You're awake." He kissed my cheek.

"I am. But I think Jamie's going to be out for the count for a bit." He'd told me that happened next.

"Why?" Reed took his turn hugging me. He squeezed my back tightly. "Is he okay?"

"Sounds like you guys started the co-joining." Thaddeus sat at the table with a knowing look in his eyes. They'd clearly all been through this. "Yes, for hours at least. Might be a day. It's a good thing."

Gage approached me, kissing the end of my nose. "Lucky bastard. Won the draw to stay with you and then gets to co-join first. I bet he cheated. I bet he somehow maneuvered those straws. He's cagey like that. Only seems like he's so sweet."

I laughed, and Krystal groaned. "Your guys are so competitive. Were they always?"

"Yes, always." I smiled as Alexander lifted me off the ground into a bear hug. "Then again so am I, so it worked perfectly."

Alexander set me down in a seat, and Reed put a plate in front of me. I took a bite of the eggs. They were utterly delicious. "Thank you," I needed Paden to know I appreciated the effort.

"It's nothing." He sat next to Krystal, taking her hand. "We're happy to help. We might be breaking rules, but then again no one gave us any."

Reed scooted into a seat next to me. "They gave me so many I couldn't tell you all of them in a single day. If they're loosening up it's just because this is truly the end. I hate that. But it reminds me of what I need to suggest."

I loved this. Strategizing was exactly what we should be doing. "What's that?"

"I think Alexander should take over One. Everyone should move up and I'll go down to Five."

I sucked in my breath. "Why's that?"

"I have a lot of history now with all the other guards everywhere. Not all of it is positive. I was pretty much in charge when we trained, and I've had to do a lot of things to keep it on track down here. I'm not going to make things easier on you. I think your future here would be better if they didn't have to deal with me."

Alexander grabbed a chair, and with a loud squeak, he scooted across the room to the table. "One problem with that brother."

"What's that?" Reed met Alexander's gaze straight on.

"Anyone who gives you shit has to get through me to do it. That's how One and Two work. Plus, you might be a problem, but you're our fucking problem. You stay One. I'm not taking it. So says Two. Not to mention all the shit I'm hearing you did to put people together. They don't like it? They can come through me."

Gage leaned against the wall. "Besides, you'd be a terrible Five. It takes a lot to keep you all in line without any of you noticing it."

Reed nodded, looking down at the floor before back up at me. "What do you want, Aspen?"

That was easy. "I want us. As we were supposed to be. Strong. Ready. I want to beat down the Darkness and then go to the ocean and spend time there, even if it's cold. A year's worth of time. I want to live long enough to see things really get better afterward."

"Then I stay One." He leaned over to kiss me. I must have been feeling really mushy because I practically melted into my chair. "And we'll go to the ocean. I love the ocean. It's fun to fly as a bird over the ocean."

"Duly noted." Ryland, one of Krystal's guards, laughed. "After the battle we're going to the ocean and we're flying over it. Speaking of that, it's been so long since we stayed human for this length of time. Kind of... I don't know."

"Itchy," Stone supplied.

That was when it dawned on me, I was the only person in the room who had never been or wasn't currently a bird. I didn't have any particular desire to fly. In fact, I was fairly certain I wouldn't like the experience at all. Now, swim through warm water on a pleasant day? Yes, that was an idea I could get behind fully.

After I killed the Darkness, I was going to the beach.

I walked to the edge of the train, the door was wide open, and I stepped out onto the platform, letting the wind hit me in the face. I raised my arms to the sky. I was power in that moment, pure undiluted, endless.

"Yes. But so am I."

I turned at the sound of the voice. The shapeless man, the shadow who walked and talked. He had no features, but his darkness matched his name. He was blacker than the night, an inked shape even against the sunless evening.

"I must be dreaming." I told him. It explained many things, actually. Like how I was here, how the train door was wide open, and where my guys were. They'd never let me be here alone without them.

"If you are, Aspen, then so am I." The Darkness took a step toward me.

Now, that was interesting. "Does Darkness dream?"

"All things with souls dream."

He had fast answers. That was always what made him and the demon in the circle, or any of them that walked this place, so appealing. The world was ending. Everything was hard. But here's an answer on a silver plate.

I might take longer to consider what I said but I had my own truths. I wasn't afraid to speak them. "You think you have a soul? If you ever did, I'd say it was long gone."

He didn't respond so fast this time. "Do you think you have one? Or did you sell it to the Sisterhood with promises of glory? Aren't you the Warrior? Aren't you destined to die?"

We circled each other, the back of the open train blowing the night air onto us. This was a dream. But it felt real, and I bet we could hurt each other if we wanted to.

I wanted to.

If he killed me in my sleep, would I die or wake?

"I'm destined to kill you. If I go, too, then so be it, but either way you're done. That's the way destiny works."

He laughed. "Little girl, I've been around so long and seen so many destinies, so many shifts in timelines, so many things that were supposed to happen that didn't, I've long since given up believing there has to be any one way or another. You are playing your role as you were meant to do. You'll die for it and nothing will change. We were both cast. Now we see which one of us knows how to survive better."

I jolted up in bed. The train swayed slowly, and the early morning light came through the window. Next to me, Jamie was as still as he'd been when I fell asleep. My heart raced and it wouldn't slow. A strong hand touched my back.

Reed. I turned into him, practically throwing myself into his lap. "I think I was really talking to the Darkness."

He rubbed circles slowly. If he was thrown by what I said to him he didn't react. His voice was low when he spoke. "We're hours from Anne's. This far in the Deadlands is old magic, real strong stuff. You might be psychically speaking to him. It's possible. But you're here. You're safe."

"Reed, who thought it could be me? Maybe you were right

all along. I'm terrified. The Warrior shouldn't be terrified. She should be strong, sure, and able. Not shaking in your arms like a leaf."

He sucked in a breath. "In retrospect, I couldn't have been more off. There isn't a Sister in the universe more qualified to do this than you. Watching you fight twice now? You move at a speed I've never seen before."

I did? I hadn't had any clue.

He wasn't done. "You are focused. Strong. You've only been at this days and they were both high level demons. Your eyes have gone completely white. You're fully in your power. A little training from some people doing with more experience and he won't stand a chance. It was my fear, not yours, that made me destroy everything."

I cupped his face in my hands and I kissed him, hard. He gasped against my mouth. "You didn't destroy anything. We're right here."

He stared at me, as though he searched my face for something. He must have found it because he nodded once. "Maybe you see in black and white when you fight because you are so full of life, of forgiveness, of color, that you can't do what you have to do in full color. As though your body knows what it has to do to pull you through."

I didn't know if that was right but I liked his explanation. For now, I was going to hold onto that. I wrapped my arms around his neck. "Thank you, Reed."

"I love you, Aspen. I always have. Always will. Come on." He lifted me from the bed. "I have an idea." He carried me into the bathroom. "There is hot water. Let's not waste time before it's gone. You know how these trains are. I'm going to draw you a bath."

Hot water was a luxury that came and went from my life. Did we really have some? A thought dawned on me. I was pretty cleaned up. How had I gotten this way? "I don't remember showering after my demon fight."

"You were asleep. We did our best to divert our eyes but we weren't going to leave you covered in demon goop." He gave me a small smile. "I realize it might be sort of invasive. It was quick and we protected your dignity as best we could. We..."

I kissed him again. "Take a bath with me."

Reed's eyes widened. "I... ah..."

I touched his lips. "Reed, did I take your words away?"

"You always do, Aspen. I won't fail you again. I'll die first."

I didn't want to think about death. There would be plenty of time for that, and I thought it would be pretty soon. If the Darkness and I communicated in my sleep, then we were probably about to tangle.

I didn't intend to lose but I wasn't going to take any time for granted either. "Enough with that. Anything can happen, right? It doesn't have to be the Darkness that gets me. Sisters die all the time, and I don't intend to dwell on it any longer."

He drew me to him, pressing my ear to his heart. "Not *my* Sister."

Reed was so sweet. It was a side of him I really only got to see. No one else was ever going to call the man that word. I touched his chin. "Bathe with me?"

He nodded fast. "Absolutely."

Reed turned on the water. I could hear it filling up the basin, but I didn't turn to look. I only had eyes for him. He was here. I was, too. What were the chances of that?

"We're both alive."

I jumped onto him. He caught me, but we both almost tumbled backward into the tub. He laughed, such a strange sound for Reed. His mouth met mine, and he kissed me. For the first time maybe ever, I had the feeling that Reed wasn't holding anything back when he met me lip-to-lip. He lived in a state of control.

He slammed me into the wall, lifting his head when he did. His eyes were huge. "Sorry."

"Don't be. I'm not fragile, just small. And I don't break." I bit down on his bottom lip. "Or at least I don't easily."

He kissed me again, hard, before pulling back to glance down at the water. "Full enough." He shut off the faucet with his foot. Reed was impressively agile. He set me down to strip me of his clothes, and I got busy doing the same to him. He was lean, his muscles well defined, but Reed had no bulk on him at all. If he wasn't so strong, he might be thin.

I wrapped my arms around his waist and kissed him right above his heart. He trembled at my caress and evidence of how much I turned him on pressed further up against me. "You're so handsome, Reed."

He shook his head. "You never wore the Sister veil and yet you see me through some sort of haze. I am not handsome. You, however, are beautiful."

He lifted me and set me down in the tub, my back to his stomach in the hot water. It wasn't scalding but warm enough that I shivered from the change in sensations. He leaned back, and I lay on him, facing away from him.

"Reed, this isn't conducive to what I want to do."

He chuckled in my ear. "It's conducive to what I want to do."

"I don't..."

His hand palmed my thigh. "Relax, Aspen. For just a minute. I want to love you. That's all."

"You do love me. Every time you do something, every time I'm in the front of your mind and you see to some need I didn't even know I had, every time you look at me. I see it. I always did. It's not different now. I can feel your love for me, Reed. I can touch it all the time."

As though speaking the words broke through whatever barrier had kept us apart, I was suddenly inside of his mind. At least this time I knew what was happening.

Reed flew through the air in his bird form. On the edge of his mind, he could feel me. If he could turn just slightly east he might even have visualization of me. I was like a warmth in his mind, but he'd never be able to turn east. Whenever he tried, invisible barriers knocked him straight to the ground. Divinity was being clear. He wasn't allowed to see me. Not even from a distance, maybe ever again.

It had been this way for decades upon decades of his existence on this miserable planet—I hadn't even been born. Getting to sense my presence now was at least some kind of gift. I lived. I breathed. He knew it. Still, the endless days of always feeling and never seeing grated on him, and he wasn't sure he could do this forever.

The end was coming. Although happiness had ended for him a long time ago.

I rushed back into my body in the bathtub. Reed's eyes were white as he regarded me silently. "Reed?"

I'd had a hard time, but he'd lived in hell. How had he made it through? Why was he...?

His mouth met mine as his hand traveled farther up my leg and he pressed a finger inside of me. Co-joining had apparently not taken him off his desired path. That was okay. I'd never complain. He found the spot inside of me that ached for him and rubbed. I sighed. Yes, by divinity, I wanted that. He found it again and with a circle played with the small bud, keeping his motions circular. I cried out into his mouth and he made the smallest sound of pleasure in the back of his throat.

The water splashed with our slightest movements. I didn't care, and I didn't think he did either. He grew incredibly hard beneath me, and yet anytime I tried to adjust to touch him he stopped me with a touch of his hand on mine.

"All about you. That's what I want. All about you." His voice strained like he was having trouble forming words. I understood the feeling.

"Reed, I want to come with you inside of me. I want a true joining. Please."

He sucked in a long breath. "Turn over, Aspen."

I did until I was on top of him. Without waiting for instruction, I stroked his hard cock once. He was halfway covered in water. I maneuvered my body until I straddled him, and then like I'd done this millions of times before, I took him inside of me. With more skill, I might have done it with less of a pinch from the joining, but I didn't care, and it quickly passed. He leaned his head back against the tub.

"Fuck."

I grinned. Was Reed using profanity? He'd really lost it. "Like that?"

"Love it. Love you." His white eyes glistened with a ferocious edge to them. Reed would never really be tamed. Contained, maybe, but there was raw power to him that had always made me want him even more.

I threaded my fingers into his hair as I started to ride him. My movements took me in and out of the water. We might have a flood by the time I was done. That was fine by me, hardly the worst thing to ever happen on a train. He leaned forward and licked the soft column of my throat. Yes, I wanted this man so much. I wanted to complete what we were doing here.

His breathing sped up, and I pushed down stronger, causing both of us to moan. He took over from the bottom. I was on top but he directed. His movements were strong and thorough. "Move with me, love."

I listened, giving him a quick nod. I'd always do whatever

Reed wanted. I always had. I never wanted to be separated. Could we stay like this forever? He sped up his jerks, and I did the same. I cried out. I was so close. Oh, so close.

One more pass and that was all it took. I exploded around him, the heat and wetness of the water only adding to the moment. I was surrounded by the sheer magnitude of Reed's love for me. I couldn't let go, wouldn't ever. He was mine, I was his. Nothing would ever come between us again.

I would see to it.

He cried out my name, and I held on, knowing what we'd started here had been created in divinity and was for all time.

WITH TWO OF MY GUYS OUT COLD, THE OTHER THREE hovered over me like I might need help breathing. If all went okay, we were an hour from the stop. I ate some soup across from Krystal and tried not to roll my eyes when Gage got up to retrieve a second napkin after I dropped one on the floor.

I would never complain about being loved too much.

"Convenient that Reed managed to get himself out of having to face the music with all the guards at Anne's." Alexander sat on the counter. "Lucky bastard."

I laughed. "I don't think it was purposeful. It's just one of those things that happens when it happens."

"Well, since I'm going to be carrying his ass in there, it seems mighty convenient to me." There was no hostility in Alexander's gaze. Really, just amusement.

"I've been thinking," Krystal interjected. "And maybe it's nothing."

She had my immediate attention. "Doubtful. What are you dwelling on, Sister Krystal?"

"You don't have to call me Sister Krystal. We're both

Sisters. I mean, I guess some Sisters do that. Never mind. Just call me Krystal, will you? Makes me feel more like friends."

Whatever she wanted. "It might take me a little bit to get used to doing that.

"Fair enough. Anyway, I was thinking about you and Anne."

I blinked. "Me and Anne? I've never met her."

I knew Krystal and Mika. I'd even encountered Teagan on more than one occasion in the other world. But Anne I'd never spoken to. She'd been a super star. We'd all known she would be in charge down here. Her soul never wavered.

"I know that, actually. I'm picturing the beginning of her journey. I don't know her that well either. Honestly, I think Daniella has the best understanding of Anne or Teagan. They're very close. They've been on this journey a long time together and their kids are of similar ages. Teagan, that is. Daniella's daughters are grown and Sisters themselves."

Children? I'd never considered the idea. It was a faraway concept. Maybe if I rid the world of the Darkness. "Go on, I'm sorry to interrupt."

She shook her head. "There are similarities to the beginning of your journey and the beginning of Anne's. For example, I know that she rescued a baby. You rescued a baby."

Thaddeus rose and poured himself some water. "You took care of a toddler."

"I know, but it strikes me as so odd that Anne saved a baby and now so has Aspen. There's a fluidity to it. If Reed were awake, he'd understand. From the point of view of the raven, you can see the ebbs and flows of things."

Gage cleared his throat. "Not to get Aspen worked up on a hot topic again, but I am usually the one who reads the futures. I was the one who saw the path that led you to Aspen and sort of arranged everything to get you on it."

Krystal's One shook his head. "If it had gone differently than it did, you'd be at risk for your life now."

Gage held up his hands. "I get it, brother. I lived with your horrifying scenario for longer than you can fathom."

Thaddeus nodded. "I know you did."

"Anne saved a young mother on a train." Krystal chewed her fingernail. "Yours died."

So maybe Anne was just a better Sister than me. "I might not be very good."

She shook her head. "No, it's not that. Gage, can you help me? I'm not clear on this."

He walked toward us. "I'm afraid I'm not following. Are you saying there is something important to the cyclical nature between Anne and Aspen? The beginning and the end?"

Krystal rose, her blonde hair falling off her shoulders and down her back. "That's what I mean, yes. Anne started what Aspen has to finish, and in between, if you take my bump out of the occasion, it's really about time, isn't it? I'm trying to understand, to read the signs that divinity has left us. I have to speak for them, and yet I'm not sure I understand it any better than any of you do. Teagan sees the past. All stages of it. She helps Anne understand what to do. And Mika is the Oracle. She finds future Sisters. Past. Future. Teagan. Mika. Anne. Aspen."

I wasn't sure if what I was going to say was going to help anything or not. I was a little bit out of my depth here. I was just the Warrior. I had to kill the Darkness. The rest seemed beyond me. "I don't know if you should count yourself out. You were hardly nothing. I mean, Mika sees new Sisters, right? You gave the planet rebirth."

She drummed her fingers on the table. "Maybe this is all just nothing. Never mind me. I'll stick to watching and telling all of you what I see from above."

The train skidded to a stop and Stone groaned. "I will not

miss being on this thing. We're here."

"You and me both."

Alexander scooted by me. "Come on, Gage, we'll go get Jamie and Reed."

The first one appeared suddenly in the doorway. "No need to get me. I'm up. I've never been better. I can grab Reed, if you want. Hi, Aspen." He rushed over to me and kissed me soundly on the lips.

I smiled up at him. "Missed you."

"Missed you, too." He pointed at his head. "But I can feel you in there and that is really something, darling."

Gage punched him in the shoulder. "Stop bragging. We'll get Reed together. Come on. Can feel her in your mind. Lucky ass."

They were all cursing a lot. I shook my head. The formality of all those years ago was long gone. I would have to try swearing myself. Alexander took my hand and with Stone beside us we left the train. The only things I had were the things in our small bags.

We exited the train into the sunshine. The conductor, a man with grayish hair and a pudge face, nodded to us. "Thank you for traveling with us, Sister, and handling the demon problem."

I might never get used to being addressed as thus. "You're welcome of course."

"It seems fitting, having you here with us today. This is the last run of the trains. The very last time we'll ever run them."

I stopped abruptly, almost stumbling forward, but Alexander caught me. I didn't understand. "I'm sorry, what?"

"This is the last run of the trains. The company has decided not to run them anymore. After today they'll be no more. You hadn't heard?"

I shook my head. "I've been involved with other things.

But that doesn't make any sense. This is an entire industry that employees a huge amount of people. It is the only way folks can get where they need to go, ever. Sure things happen." I knew better than most. "That doesn't mean it can be shut down."

He looked away from me, emotion evident in his face. "Thank you, Sister. That's what we've been saying. Still, this is it. The last train and it's almost to nowhere."

Stone drew me down, and I followed onto the train platform. The last train. The final one. To almost nowhere.

Twelve of us were on the platform, eleven of us watching as the conductor exited. Had we been the very final passengers, truly?

It really was the end of days.

I touched Reed's unconscious form to assure myself he breathed as Gage and Alexander brought him to a cart nearby. They'd wheel him to the Sisterhood, which would be easier. We had a small town to pass through before we reached Anne's. I'd done this walk twice.

I supposed I'd always remember where I'd been the last time a train ran.

"Endings and beginnings." I spoke aloud to hear my own voice. There was more to this. I just didn't know what yet.

ANNE'S SISTERHOOD STOOD OUT IN THE DISTANCE. A LARGE house that had once been a schoolhouse, it had been knocked down and rebuilt several times. The brothels were always filled with stories of men being called in to fix it. In fact, if I wasn't wrong, it was on one of those occasions that Mika had met her husbands. Divinity did have its way.

"He's unconscious so I suppose I can't ask Reed how he arranged to get all the guards here."

From a distance, the Sisterhood looked busy. The gate opened and closed. Men and women marched in and out and a bell rang slowly. It was almost dinnertime. Was that what the ding signaled?

A woman walked out. I recognized her immediately. She'd been part of my last rescue from Katrina. A second later five women followed, quickly after her. The first woman hurried to me.

Her name was Beth. She had long brown hair and blue eyes. "Aspen, everyone's been waiting."

"That's my cue." Krystal hugged my side before she nodded at Beth and took off, shifting to a bird.

"Wait," I called up to her. "You're leaving?"

She didn't answer me, disappearing with five black birds following in her wake.

Beth laughed. "There are rules about what she can and can't do. That's what Teagan says anyway. Everyone is glad you're here, finally."

"Beth," one of the women following her called out to her. "It's not safe out here."

The other woman nodded. "They love me." Her cheeks blushed a pretty shade of red. "Never want me to be hurt. If only they knew all the things I did before they showed up to protect me. Claudia, this is the woman who saved my life. I wouldn't be here at all without her."

Claudia rushed toward me, ready to grab me when Alexander stepped in front of her. "I don't touch your Sister without permission. You don't touch mine."

They stared at each other for a second. Finally, the woman spoke. "Sounds fair. I was going to hug her and say thank you."

Beth groaned. "Let's leave them to it. They have what they're good at, we have what we are. Welcome home, Aspen. From what Teagan has seen in her visions, it's about time."

❧ 7 ❧

Anne's Sisterhood looked like a description of organized chaos. One time, when I hadn't been able to find a job cleaning a brothel or a bar, I'd taken some time sorting tin in a factory. That had been a little bit like this. People were all over the place, but everyone knew where they were going. Guards trained in the center of the courtyard.

Several of them stopped when they saw us, probably looking for Reed, because when they saw him out cold they'd go back to what they were doing. A lot of them grinned while several others scowled. Co-joining really seemed to be a thing that triggered a response.

Following my gaze, Beth sighed. "Not every guard has a Sister and vice versa. Anne is determined not to assign guards that aren't matched to Sisters. It's complicated. Honestly, in just the days he's been gone I think everyone is missing Reed. Krystal is not around to play matchmaker. Divinity seems to have tasked her with helping with the final battle."

"He'd be surprised to hear that." I looked over my

shoulder to where Alexander was bringing Reed to a guest-house. "He doesn't feel exactly beloved."

"It's complicated, right? All I know is that Reed brought my ladies to me. I didn't know I could have what my heart wanted. And once I was free of Katrina he saw that it happened."

That begged a question. "Now that everyone is free of Katrina, what is happening to the Sisters who were with her until the end, either by choice or because they were prisoners?"

Going there and helping them would have been something I would have done when I was a human. Now I had my own journey and no trains running to get there.

"That's complicated, too. Anne sent some Sisters out to help. She's doing the best she can. This has all been a logistical nightmare. Daniella is going to take over the running of the day-to-day now that you're here."

Her words opened my mind to the truth. I shuddered. "Because I am the bringer of death? My arrival means the end."

"Your arrival means there is a chance." Teagan rose from where she sat on the ground. "Hello, Aspen. We don't know each other. I'm Teagan."

I took her hand in mine and squeezed. "We did know each other. In another place. And maybe you feel like you know me because you've seen me in your visions?"

Her smile was slow. It had to be hard to live two different lives. One in the present, one in the what once was, and still manage to function in the now. "I don't have my complete memories of that other time. Do you?"

"I never lost them."

Her eyes widened. She was beautiful. Blonde hair, blue eyed, like a pixie in some ways. She was also tough as nails. I didn't know Teagan's whole story from this life, but I'd heard enough to know she endured what would have killed others. One of her guards came over to her, placing his hand on her back. He wore an eyepatch.

He addressed not me, but Alexander, who had just arrived back to us. "Good to have you here, at last. Where have you been forever? And Reed is out. I see Jamie co-joined. All good news. We need you guys strong."

A muscle ticked in Alexander's jaw. "I've been to the pits of hell and back. Sorry if my arrival took a little longer. We had to, you know, manipulate time and destiny without destroying anyone's life." I reached out to touch his cheek. He leaned into my fingers, slightly. This was why Reed was One. Alexander had no capacity to refrain from wanting to deck anyone who spoke to us. I had no idea why, but he took every conversation as a threat to me. "I imagine we'll co-join whenever that happens."

Jamie stepped forward next to him. "It happens when it happens. As Thaddeus here obviously did, he must know that."

Teagan put her hands on her hips. "Thaddeus, I could really do without the machismo today. You want to go play 'who handles the sword better' with Reed when he wakes up, you can feel free to do that, but let's not poke at the bear while they're so obviously in upheaval not completely co-joined yet. You remember that feeling, my love? Like every minute everything might implode."

Thaddeus gave her a slow grin, full of hidden words neither one of them was speaking aloud. I wasn't great at reading people but even I could see that. "I remember lots of things about that. Sure, I'll wait for Reed. We'll see if he's still the best of us or if his years of cushy flying around took away his fighting skills."

"Don't talk about my One like that." Stone spoke from behind us. I'd never been so aware of my guys' numbers as I was right then. Threes were there to take the fall for Ones and Twos. Stone had always been happy to throw himself on the line for any of them.

I cleared my throat. "We are all on the same side, right?"

Teagan met my gaze, lifting her eyebrows. "You and I are. The Sisters are here for each other. The guards are a different situation. We tried for a while but then it became clear to us that their goals are not the same as ours. You and I have universal objectives that have to do with saving the world. They are here for us. Not for any other reason. My guys would leave and turn their back on this whole mess if I wanted to. I bet yours would, too. We are their ultimate goal. Everything and anything that isn't them is a threat to us."

Well, that was going to get downright exhausting.

I didn't know that my guys would walk away from it all. They'd spent endless years on this project. They were going to see it through. I turned, waiting for one of them to disagree.

Gage shrugged. "Want to go? We can go. If that's an option, I'm happy to take it. Go find somewhere near an ocean and wait out our days, just the six of us..."

I rolled my eyes at him, and he smiled. He had to be kidding, right?

Anne rounded the corner heading straight for us. She had five guys hurrying with her. Her smile was warm and welcoming. "You're here. Just right on the timeline Teagan said."

"You'd think I had visions or something." She winked at me. There were so many conversations being held in this place that were nonverbal. I was going to have to adjust to that.

Anne groaned before she took my arm. "We're all new to you, I think. We have to go find Mika and you've seen Krystal. You know them. And Beth. So I guess we're not all new to you, here?"

Beth took a step back, nodding to me. Her women followed after her, wherever they were going. My own guards weren't far behind me. Were they about to have another bad interaction with Anne's guards? They all seemed fine. Teagan's guys hurried along with us, not at all thrown by the Alpha pushback thing they'd just done. My own men seemed unrattled as well.

Was I just going to get used to the idea that they might all explode into anger at any time or was this a line that they played around but wouldn't cross? Men were confusing to me.

"We need to have a meeting. Ones only, otherwise the room gets too crowded, and we talk about what to do now." She looked up at the circling birds in the sky. I'd not noticed them before, but there had to be at least one hundred of them. Anne called out, "You can come, Krystal, if it's appropriate."

Anne shook her head when there was no response from Krystal. "So glad you're here and you're you. I don't know your whole story. But it sounds like you've been through the ringer."

I was going to end up being such a disappointment. "I don't know that I'm going to save the day. And my One is out of commission at the moment. He's..."

"Hey," Reed cried out, catching up to us. His presence in my mind flared to life. He must have just woken up and darted out here. He grabbed onto my arm. "I'm here. Don't go anywhere without me."

"Reed," several of the guards spoke his name, but he ignored their presence. "You okay, my love?"

"I am." It was good to see his eyes open, even if they were now white. Some of the other guards seemed to be able to switch their eye color back and forth. I'd seen Thaddeus do it twice now. We needed to figure that out. I missed their eye color. "My One is available."

Alexander nodded to all of us. "We'll go get set up. I'm looking for equipment. Be on alert, Reed. Some of these idiots seem to think they can kick your ass."

Reed snorted. "That so? I've been watching them for quite a while. Maybe it's a discomfort in knowing I know all their secrets, where all their bodies are buried, so to speak."

"Maybe I just want to know if it still is as it once was," Bryant, Anne's One, spoke for the first time. "But there will be time for that and it's not now."

Alexander's grin was huge. "Love you, Aspen. See you soon."

I didn't know why that second we co-joined. The others had been in intimate situations. But he was just so Alexander in that moment. There was nothing he wasn't sure he could conquer, nothing that intimidated him ever, not even Reed, and he lived life on his own terms. I loved him so completely for just being him.

I was suddenly deep in his memory. There was a loud buzzing and I, as Alexander, walked quickly through what had to be the old Sisterhood. It was nighttime and there weren't a lot of people around but I couldn't be caught, regardless. This was breaking the law of divinity. If I was found it would all go to hell.

I wouldn't allow that. Not ever. Not when Aspen was on the line.

I'd failed her—me—once. I'd never do it again. Beelzebub was right where he was supposed to be. Now I just needed him to notice Krystal so that the other powers that were here could do the same. Take note. I shifted into my bird body and flew at her window. Several times I banged it. The old demon hated things that disrupted the norm. A raven banging a window would catch his attention. He would at least want to know what was inside that made me act so strangely.

Or at least that was the hope.

This was going to hurt like a motherfucker.

But I'd do anything for Aspen.

I rushed the window. Bang.

I jolted back into my body. There were people all around us but it felt like it was just Alexander and me in the universe. His eyes were white and he was right there in my mind where he had somehow always been. Steady Alexander, who feared nothing and loved me so much he would endure any physical pain for me, always.

I marched toward him and took him in my arms. "Don't hurt yourself. Am I clear? I don't want you to have any more pain. Not for me."

He whispered in my ear, his breath a warm caress on my cheek. "There is no amount of pain that I wouldn't take on to have you. There is nothing that having you wouldn't be worth. Now, I've got to say. This is not how I hoped to co-join. It is so... nice to be there with you. Like I'm wondering how I ever did without it. As though I can finally breathe. But when I wake up from whatever this bullshit passing out thing is, I want you in my bed so I can feel you naked beneath me."

My whole body had to be bright red. Everyone would know what we were talking about and with my link, the other two they certainly knew.

Jamie laughed. Yep, they knew.

Privacy was apparently a thing of the past.

I whispered back in his ear. "Find me when you get up. I'll... show you how much I love you."

He kissed my cheek, lingering there. "Be safe, Aspen."

For twenty-four years he hadn't been able to protect me. I could now feel how that weighed on him. "I won't go anywhere without you."

Maybe I finally understood why the guards followed us

around so closely. And why they were willing to fight each other just for speaking to us.

Even if I was going to see if I could put a stop to it. Eventually.

Movement out of the corner of my eye caught my attention as my powers buzzed to life, taking me by surprise. I wasn't alone. All of the Sisters seemed to jolt with electricity. I gasped. I'd thought the demon I fought on the train tracks was big, but he had nothing on the one in front of me. I pushed Anne behind me. She was pivotal, and this one had to be working with the Darkness directly. I was never going to beat him, but I had to try and...

"Aspen, it's okay." Alexander held me back. "It's Beelzebub. He's not a good guy, but he's been here a long time with the Sisters. He lives here. They don't fight him. He... unwittingly helped with Krystal."

Mika strode toward us, her hair blowing everywhere in the wind. She'd never looked better. The woman practically glowed. When last I'd seen her, she'd been under the abuse of Katrina and been practically on death's door. "We call him Bob. The demon Bob. I'm not sure he cares for it. But we do it anyway."

"Little passive aggressive happiness." Teagan shrugged. "If you give it a second, your powers will shut down." Anne let out a long breath. "Helps to breathe through it. Divinity knows we leave this one alone."

The demon stared down at me. He was bigger than the house. I swallowed. Fear crept through me, and I knew my three connected would feel it. I hated that they would know just what a coward I was. How I reacted like this to every demon I encountered, how they had been right that I wasn't ready to be the Warrior.

I might as well turn around and tell Stone and Gage right now. Just get it out there.

The demon stared down at me. Other Sisters' powers might be calming down but my own still rode me hard.

"You are smart." The demon spoke to me, and it took me a moment to register what he'd said. Should I be flattered? Was I supposed to respond? He kept speaking before I could. "You have a tendency to stick your nose into things that you should best leave alone. That's why you might win this. They chose well. Darkness to light. Always so much bullshit."

That was right. It was what happened to bring Sisters fully into their powers. I still had to suffer. I made my knees stay steady. I couldn't show weakness in front of this demon. "I bet you could take it out. Why don't you just end the Darkness?"

The demon shook his head. "Why don't you ask the Sister Superior that sometime when you are dead? Oh, that's right. You're going to vanish. You won't get to do that. I'm going to sleep now. If you let my world end I'll make it so apocalypse feels like a vacation."

With that, he seemed to shrink and fade, disappearing under the main house. My powers cooled, leaving me shaky. I'd never refrained from using them before when they shot to life. "Does he just live here? Under the house? You made your home here?"

"There are lots of ironies in our life." Anne sighed. "Come on. Meeting still back on. That was practically a nod he gave you, Aspen. He thinks you can do it."

I didn't know if I wanted the endorsement of a demon. But the ladies here seemed to like him. At the very least, they weren't afraid. I turned to Gage and Stone. We hadn't co-joined yet, but I didn't care for them any less than the other three. It was important they understood what was happening. "Ask Jamie to tell you how I felt just then. You need to know. I... I don't want you to make a mistake in thinking I'm one way when I'm really quite different."

They looked at each other and then at me. Stone opened and closed his mouth, but then he nodded and stepped back. Jamie's love pulsed through our connection. He didn't like that I'd just done that. Did he want to protect me from myself? That was too bad. I owned my weaknesses.

We entered the house, the building well-constructed on the inside. Low electric light created a whining sound in the kitchen. Electricity came and went from my life. Sometimes we'd had it, sometimes we hadn't. That was okay. I knew how to use it to my advantage and how to deal quite well when it went away.

Like the trains, it was something we likely wouldn't have very much longer.

Anne brought us all into a room that had a long table and seats for a dozen people. I took my cue from the others, sitting down in a seat around the corner while our Ones stayed back by the walls. I glanced back at Reed and he nodded at me. He was okay. I could feel it. If the aggression from the others bothered him, he wasn't showing it in our link.

Krystal hadn't appeared to join us but an older woman was there. I'd never met her and was thinking I really should introduce myself when she leaned across the table and offered me her hand. "I'm Daniella, child. Welcome to the fight. I guess you are our weapon."

"I guess I am." She must be the Daniella who Beth said was going to take over things. Beth wasn't in here with us now. It was Mika, Daniella, Anne, Teagan and myself. The Oracle, Sister Superior, The Prophet, The Warrior, and whatever Daniella turned out to be. I tried to remember her. There were so many Sisters in the other place. We'd all been young there. I shook my head. Like Anne, I might never have known her.

Anne stood at the head of the table. "When we found out

you'd been given powers, Aspen, I started to imagine this day. I guess that wasn't very long ago but every hour since has felt like a lifetime. You're here. You're the Warrior. It is time."

I was supposed to say something. That much I quickly gathered. "I'm not shy so it's not hard for me to figure out how to say this, it's just hard for me to admit because I am, in fact, prideful. I'm not a very good Warrior. I fought two demons so far and neither one of them has been particularly smooth."

Teagan nodded. "You've only had powers for days. Not even a full week. We all had years to practice. You've taken out two demons, and you're not dead or delusional. I'd say it's a win."

"Be that as it may, as Anne has pointed out, we're toward the end. I've had contact with the Darkness. In my sleep. I am not in any way equipped to beat anything right now. I need to get trained, as much as I can for as long as I can, if I'm to do this. Also, the trains are not running, so we should assume that the fight will be right here."

Mika nodded. "We've always heard that the last battle would be here. I've stopped having visions. There are no new Sisters coming. We are it. The ones here are with us are the last ones."

"My visions are halted," Teagan added. "The last things I saw were about you, Aspen. I've seen all I can see. What we can do now is train and wait. Divinity will tell Krystal if there is something she can share. She's here to help, but like Reed before her, she's limited. There are walls that stop her from doing certain things."

I expected Reed to comment, but he didn't. "I do have some questions."

"Go ahead." Anne nodded. "You must have so much you don't understand. You were in our world but not really. Not since birth. There are some things that are just different here."

To say the least. I cleared my throat. "Krystal gave me her powers and yet I don't have her powers. She rebirthed the planet. I couldn't do that. I can kill demons. She couldn't do that, not like I can. How is that?"

"Powers are part of who we are." Daniella told me. "They come into the very essence of us and become a tool for us like any other tool. Powers were one thing with Krystal's soul and another for you. Power is one thing for her and a different entity for you."

"So at its essence power is the same then? Your power? My power? Teagan's power?"

Daniella nodded. "That is how I understand it. They gift us power, and it changes depending on who receives the gift. Why are you interested in this? I'm happy to talk about power all day but it seems that isn't what you would be focused on. Don't you want to talk about fighting?"

"This is a man—a being—who has spent his entire existence since he died possessing a powerful Sister and other powerful humans to bring forth Armageddon. Beelzebub can't touch him. Divinity hasn't sent a lightning strike to knock him dead." I realized as I spoke the words this was the part of all of this that I'd never really grasped. As Aspen the initiate I'd never questioned it; as Aspen the fallen Sister I'd not had time to consider it, But now as the Warrior? I couldn't let this go. "I think this isn't a question of whose abilities are stronger, of who is better at wielding magic, at who can dissolve to the cellular level and reemerge victorious. I think this is about understanding powers. His. Mine. The Universe."

Anne nodded at me. "I think you're right. So let's make you as powerful as you can be. For tonight, get some rest, get some food, get ready. Tomorrow, I'll teach you as I was taught. Teagan will do the same. Mika. Daniella. We'll teach you until the battle comes. And we'll figure out the power."

I nodded at her, but even as I did, I knew that wasn't the right answer. The problem was I couldn't figure out the right question to ask. I just didn't know what I didn't know.

❧ 8 ❧

I wandered around the Sisterhood with Stone. Eventually, I found my way into the library of the guesthouse. It was stacked ceiling to floor with books about demons and the Sisterhood. I could read a little bit, which was more than a lot of people who came out of the same circumstances I did. Sisters had extreme education, even under Katrina. They were all more than literate. I was behind the eight ball in that regard, too.

I pointed at the books. "Can you read, Stone?"

He nodded his head. "I retained that knowledge from the transition. You could read in the other dimension, too. Can you here?"

I shook my head. "My memory doesn't extend like that. It's so weird. I can read. A little bit. But only what I learned here which is not much."

My cheeks heated up. This was one of those things I really didn't like about myself. Stone touched my arm. "Jamie told us what you were feeling, what you wanted him to tell us. Did you think we'd think less of you for feeling afraid? Or that I would now because you can't read?"

I didn't know how to answer that without feeling like a fool because the answer he already disdained was the truth. Yes, I did. "Are you going to ever tell me how you got hurt?"

I referred to the scar on his face. He reached up to touch it. "Avoidance?"

"I'm the best at it." I sighed. "Yes, I expect you to think less of me for both of those reasons, because I think less of me. How's that?"

Stone dragged me to him, pulling me gently to his body. His mouth came down on mine. I gasped at the caress. It was so not like Stone to initiate affection. I closed my mouth and followed his lead. This was heaven. He pushed me against the bookshelf and pulled back, breathing heavily.

"Being afraid and doing it anyway: that's called courage. Not being afraid when it's appropriate to be? That's called stupid."

I laughed. I couldn't help myself. He was right. But the way he put things? I loved it. I nodded. "You're right. I'm not good at seeing things that way. It just feels like failure."

"I saw a girl. Maybe four years old. About to be possessed. I intervened. I couldn't help myself. I know that's against the rules. If we're not guards, we can't help. I got burned." He pointed to his cheek. "Is it ugly? Is that why you haven't co-joined with me?"

My heart fell into my stomach. "What? No, of course not. I'm not in control of that. It's not ugly. You're gorgeous. And I would never feel that way."

He nodded. "I guess I have my own insecurities. I can't be judging yours."

I touched his long scar. "Does it hurt?"

"Sometimes. But most of the time it's totally numb. I ignore it. It's a reminder I can't change the future alone. And it's a memory of a terrible time, a horrible event. A reminder of the truth of the world we live in."

I ran my thumb down the length of it. "I would have killed that demon."

"I know. You are so amazing. Like my own personal magic maker." His eyes flared. "You were doing things for the world even when you had no power. You're brave. If you're doing it loaded with fear, I don't care two shits about it. And if there's something you want read that you can't, I'll read it to you."

I moved my hand from his scar to trace the length of his nose. "What do you think about having sex with me in a place that someone could walk into? Like a library?"

A second later I was flat on my back on the table. My head hit a book before Stone flung it away. I winced. Books had always seemed like sacred texts to me, mostly because of my struggle reading them. My attention quickly turned back to Stone.

His mouth came down on mine. My nipples hardened, and I knew what I wanted more than anything in the world was Stone inside of me. I needed him; he was a missing piece of my heart. The world wouldn't feel right until we were connected in every possible way.

I didn't need air. I just needed him.

We undressed each other slowly. Considering the possibility that anyone could come through the door at any time, we were actually unhurried. To be fair, most people were sleeping which was what we should have been doing, too. This was much more fun.

Stone's blond hair fell into his eyes. He'd always been so beautiful, and despite his worry that hadn't changed. If anything, the gentleness of his features were more striking against the rugged scar. A scar that showed he wouldn't stand inactive while someone suffered.

I ran my hands over his chest, finding the dusting of hair there soft under my fingers. "You're beautiful, Stone."

"Stop. You're the beautiful one."

The contrast between my black hair and his blonde caught my attention. I didn't know why staring at the two colors together had caught my eye, but for a second I couldn't take my eyes off the contrast. Stone made the world brighter. He always had.

We kissed again. And then again, our bodies intertwining like our hair had earlier until we were tangled in each other. He took my breasts in his mouth, and I sucked on his neck. He tasted like salt and like maleness. I wanted to mark him, and I bit down.

He cried out, his body jerking against mine. "Aspen, you kill me. I'm trying to be slow with you. To make sure you enjoy this."

"I don't need slow." I needed him out of his own head and here with me.

That seemed to do the trick. He hauled me over until I was on top of him and he lay on the table. "You on top of me, that's how I want it."

Then that was how I wanted it, too. I positioned myself on top of him until I straddled his body. Taking his cock in my hands, I stroked him twice from balls to tip. He flared his nostrils but otherwise kept his body very still.

A muscle ticked in his jaw. He was holding back. I could always tell when Stone was on the edge of losing it in a fight. This looked very similar. He was holding on by a thin edge. He fisted his hands.

I wasn't going to make him wait. We'd had too long apart as it was. I took him deep inside of me, pressing down as quickly as I could. He was big, and my muscles had to stretch to accommodate him. Once I had him deep inside, it was heaven.

He stared up at me, his eyes huge. "Nothing in existence could ever be better than this."

I smiled down at him. "Stone." Sometimes just saying his name was enough.

"It feels like I finally came home."

I moved slowly up and down, taking him as deep as I could. In this position, I controlled where and how his cock stroked me. My clit was swollen, and each pass sent thunderbolts of pleasure through my body. Or at least that's how it felt.

Sweat broke out all over me. I might have exploded from the heat we generated together. I slowed down only to speed back up again. Stone bit down on his lip; the muscles in his neck visibly strained. He was holding off for me.

I needed to come.

And I knew just how that was going to happen.

I grabbed his hand, pressing his finger inside of me as we moved. "Touch me. Please. Right there. Just... press..."

He did as I asked, and it was all that I needed. I didn't so much come as I shattered into a million pieces around him. Or maybe it just felt that way. Did it matter? For a second, I only existed because Stone did.

He called out my name, and I was in his mind.

Still reeling from what we did in the real world, the co-joining took me by surprise. I gasped but only I could hear it. As it was, Stone walked down a long hallway. Gage was at his side. I couldn't see so much as feel his frown inside of me. Stone was pissed. Like always, he was holding back his emotions. If he didn't, he'd never get through the day.

As Stone, I rushed to a fountain of water. I knew what that was. It was the place where Sister Superior could see all our fates, the many possibilities of all of humankind. We were not supposed to be in here. Brother Raven could sometimes attend as he had the ability to move in and out of dimensions, but regular guards were not invited to the fountains. At least not unattended, and the two of them were clearly alone.

"Find the path, Gage. There has to be one. I won't lose Aspen. I'll end my guard existence and find her as a human before I never see her again."

Gage shook his head. "They could send you down in a different time all together or do something fucked up and make you her grandfather. Don't put that past them. The fact that they'd send her down powerless to begin with..."

I knew Gage was right, but I hated it—and him—just a little bit for being true. I wasn't supposed to be here. I was supposed to be on Earth watching Aspen from the moment we were born until she took her powers and beat the Darkness. I needed to make sure she was safe. I loved her, and I'd let her down completely. This wasn't the end of us, I simply couldn't exist in a universe where that was the case.

Gage whistled through his teeth. "How willing are you to manipulate and maneuver others to make this happen?"

"One hundred percent willing. There's nothing I won't do."

I was thrown back into my body, falling down onto Stone's hard chest. He wrapped me up in his arms, and I lifted my head just to confirm what I already knew. His eyes were white. They were. He smiled up at me.

"I needed this. You'll never know how much."

Actually I did. Because now that I had him in deep in my mind, I wasn't sure how I'd existed without him there.

"You're going to pass out." I kissed his chin. "Better get you to a bed."

"For many reasons. You wore me out, woman."

I grinned at him. He was my Stone and for as long as I existed, we'd be together. I'd see to it.

WITH THE MOON HIGH IN THE SKY, I YAWNED. I SHOULD

have been asleep hours before. I'd never had a great sleep, wake cycle and that hadn't changed since becoming a Sister. Passing out from exertion didn't seem like it was great, restful sleep.

Gage came over to where I stood by the window of the guesthouse. "You need to rest."

"I know. But the last time I slept I was visited by the Darkness. It has put me off the idea."

He kissed the back of my neck. "He can visit all he wants. Just seems the act of a desperate being who knows his days are numbered."

I wished I shared his vision. "I'm not so sure, Gage."

"I had to be last to co-join. I knew it right away when Krystal's guys explained it to us. The meeting of the minds. You're going to see things about me you won't like."

I turned in his arms to face him. "The insecurities among the five of us could fill the whole Sisterhood. We are a wrecked bunch of people. Well, maybe not Alexander. He's pretty sure of himself. The rest of us are walking balls of self-esteem problems."

Gage smiled, which was what I wanted, but the worry didn't leave his gaze. "I'm serious."

"Tell me before I see it." That seemed the best way to manage that anxiety. "Just own it and we'll talk it out."

He nodded. "I would have done anything to bring you back where you belonged. Anything. I knew there was a possibility Krystal died. I didn't know that she was going to be this new role, that she'd be fine. I didn't know that. I didn't tell the others. I did it anyway."

I wasn't sure why he thought I didn't know that. "Yes."

"I did that. I made the decision. And I know you aren't going to like that. You're going to be in my head and you're going to see that I am the kind of person who would sacrifice anything and everything for you. Aspen, you have lines you don't cross. I don't have them. Not when it comes to you."

I kissed him squarely on the mouth. "Gage, you are not telling me anything I don't know. I'm fully aware that you were willing to throw Krystal to the wolves to bring back me. Fortunately, that didn't happen, so we are not living with that. Am I thrilled? No. Would I do anything for you, and I mean anything, yes I would. Whatever lines you think I have, I don't."

There, I'd told him the truth. We were two imperfect people willing to do horrible things if it came down to it for the people we loved. He seemed to visibly relax, some of the stiffness in Gage's back relaxing. "You were mine to love and care for. I let you down in the worst possible way."

"I let you down, too. I should have told you from day one who I was meant to be. I lied by omission. I guess we're both guilty of those things. We've paid for our mistakes. Krystal forgives us. If there is reckoning from divinity later, we'll take it. Let's not wreck what little time we might have. I may not always like everything you do, but I like who you are, Gage. I love you."

He pulled me into his arms. I expected to co-join right there but given that I'd not been in control of any of it from day one, the jolt didn't happen. Maybe I was just too tired. He picked me up. "Come on. I'm going to put you to bed. I'll stay with you. You can sleep knowing you're in my arms."

When I didn't object, he brought me into one of the guest rooms and laid me down on the bed. A thought dawned on me. "They gave us this entire guest house. Did they oust someone from where they were living to do this?"

"We can only control so many things. The living arrangements are not on us. Leave that to whoever does that. We'd move if someone needed this more. I think you're pretty important right now. Destined to battle and all that."

I crawled underneath the covers. They were warm, and they smelled clean. Gage crawled in next to me, wrapping his feet around mine. I pressed my face into his chest, listening to his heartbeat. It was steady and rhythmic. At some point, he must have fallen asleep because his breathing changed, becoming deeper. Long breaths from the bottom of his lungs, let out slowly.

I forced myself to close my eyes. I wasn't going to be able to do anything if I didn't get some real sleep. Even bad sleep had to be better than none.

Gage's arms tightened around me.

I didn't know how long I'd been asleep when a noise woke me. I came awake, jerking in the bed so strongly I woke Gage. He was immediately alert.

"Babe?" He looked left and right.

I stared at the walls. The shadows moved, forming the figure of a man. "You see that, right? I'm not asleep, right? You are awake, too?"

"We're both awake, my love. Demon?"

"Yes and no. That's the Darkness." I grabbed onto his arm. "Get out of here. Go get the Sisters. Tell them the battle has started."

Gage banged on the wall three times, hard. "I'm not leaving you. Not for half a second."

"This is touching." The Darkness had the same voice as he'd had during my dream, which at least confirmed that I hadn't made it all up in a delusional dream. That had happened. "He loves you. This isn't the end. We won't battle now. This is just a warning. You will meet me tomorrow night at sunset outside the gates. You will come and do this or I will kill one of you every night until you show up. One Sister every night."

Fury drove me to sit up straight. "I'm not a coward. I

don't have to be threatened. You won't kill anyone. That's not how this works. I kill you."

"Do you? Have you ever killed anyone, Aspen?"

He disappeared, dissolving into the shadows. Reed burst through the door with more force than necessary just as I threw my arms around Gage. My mind twisted, jumping into Gage's with more force than I'd ever had in a co-joining.

We weren't in a plotting memory or a battle. The sun shone down on Gage as he sat next to me by a lake in the other dimension. A purple haze covered everything, and I leaned over to place my head on his shoulder. He sighed, kissing my hair and breathing me in.

The sound of a river running into the lake filled the air around us but otherwise everything was quiet. Still, he kept his hand on his side as though he might need his sword. Gage was always ready to battle for me against anything and anyone. Even in this place. As far as he was concerned there was no such thing as safe, not when it came to me.

I was thrown back into my own mind. Gage made the slightest moan in the back of his throat before he lifted his head to look at Reed. "The Darkness was here."

"I heard the last part of his speech. You're both okay? Good job getting help. Almost hope you knock out and wake up fast. If we're battling, it will be rough without you."

Gage rubbed his head on my shoulder. "The timing could be better. But as has been pointed out to me, I wasn't in control of the when. Neither was she. What happens when I knock out? Do you remember?"

"Not a thing." Reed walked over to me then sat on the edge of the bed. "Stone, Alexander, and Gage all unconscious as you go into battle with the Darkness. Feels like the odds are stacked against us."

The odds had never been particularly great to begin with. "Look, we've been defying odds from day one of this. I'm not supposed to have powers. Let's not give up hope just yet. Let's see what happens."

Reed rose. "I'm going to fill Jamie in. I'll see you in a little bit. Go back to sleep if you can. Now more than ever we need you rested." Reed squeezed Gage's shoulder. "I'll stay close in case anything happens again. I was across the building. Sorry it took me too long to get here."

Gage shook his head. "Maybe thirty seconds."

"A lifetime." Reed shut the door behind him.

Gage kissed me, softly. "I didn't know what was about to happen there. I'm glad it's over. I'm even gladder to be in there." He touched my head, gently. "You really do love me as much as you say you do."

I got up on my knees. "Gage, I have oodles of adrenaline running through my body right now. I'm in fight or flight. I know this feeling. It happened every time I invaded the Sisterhood. I... Would it be all right if I got on your lap and we just went at it like that? I'm not being articulate about this. I..."

He pulled me onto his lap. "Are you kidding? Whatever you want and you don't have to feel obligated to if you're not in the mood..."

"Check our link. Am I not in the mood?" I was probably going to be dead at sunset the next day. The door flung open and Alexander strode in.

We both turned to look at him. He stood in the doorway. "You guys okay? I woke up to blasts of terror and then Reed says we're in deep shit."

Gage crooked his finger. "Come love her with me."

My heart stuttered. Together? Were they serious? The thought had never dawned on me. Maybe it should have, but it wasn't something people talked about in the Sisterhood. Alexander crawled up behind me, leaning down to kiss my shoulder blade. "Only if you want to.

Tell me to go and I'll go. Won't even have my feelings hurt."

"I... I'm game if you two are."

Gage kissed the other side of my neck. "We haven't planned this. It might take a few minutes to figure out some of the logistics."

I swallowed. "By all means, experiment on me."

If I was going out, I was going out with a bang that was for sure.

They took off my clothes. For all that they said they were going to have to sort this out, they were rather good at working together. That shouldn't be surprising. They'd always worked well together as a team.

Alexander tended to plow through things and Gage followed up, making sure all angles were handled. They were doing the same with me.

Gage watched while Alexander finished undressing me. He lifted his gaze to mine, speaking to me even as he addressed Gage.

"I think she's even more beautiful here than she was up there."

My heart sped. "We didn't have sex up there, Alexander. Not really. It was different. All energy, sort of."

Gage laughed, a low sound. "Doesn't mean we weren't imagining it. The physical might not have had the same impact, but we knew that it could. Trust me. We wanted you. End of story."

I couldn't pretend I didn't know what they meant. I'd had the same thoughts. "What now?"

Alexander laid me down on the bed, sticking me between them until I faced Gage, with him on my back. "Now you let us love you."

He kissed my shoulder, making his way down my back, ever so slowly. Goosebumps broke out on my skin. Somehow,

I hadn't thought Alexander would be a gentle lover and yet he treated me with the utmost tenderness. Gage leaned over, taking my nipple in his mouth.

Between the warmth of Alexander's lips on my back and Gage's strong pull on my nipple I could have come right there from the intensity alone. My body shuddered. Alexander's hand came, massaging my ass before giving it a strong squeeze. I loved the pinch of pain. He smoothed his hand over where he had grabbed me.

I sighed against him. "I don't know what to do with my hands."

Gage lifted his mouth. "Put them over your head."

"But then I can't touch either of you."

Alexander whispered in my ear. "You can, later. But, yes, for now, keep your hands to yourself, my love. This is us. Fucking you."

CHAPTER NINE

9

Alexander's rough wording surged through me like he'd stroked my clit with his hands. I throbbed. Yes, they wanted to fuck me? They could do that as much and for as long as they wanted to. Alexander kissed my neck. "We need to do this faster than we'd have liked. Gage is going to go under, and we can't have that happen too soon or it will be awkward in the middle of things. So you'll have to excuse us if we don't linger on the foreplay. I'd have loved to do the foreplay."

They were new to their bodies and yet they acted like they knew what they were doing. Maybe they'd had the same sort of imaginings I'd had over the years.

Alexander pressed a finger inside of me, finding my clit and stroking it. I cried out. It took him a second to figure out my rhythm. He didn't immediately know he should use a circular motion. But he caught on fast, and as Gage made love to my breasts, I tried to keep my hands over my head as instructed.

It was hard not to touch them but not difficult to let them love me. That was what they were doing.

Alexander looked up at Gage. "Ready?"

"More than." Gage's voice sounded rough. He scooted slightly toward me, and I could feel his hard cock against my leg. Yes, I'd say he was ready.

Alexander moved his hand as Gage adjusted his position. I couldn't stand the no touching thing and dropped my hands so I could hold onto his shoulders.

Behind me, Alexander sighed and then laughed. "I'm going to play with your breasts while he takes you, gorgeous, because, yeah, they're yours, and I'm obsessed with them."

This was somehow just right. Gage quiet and all seeing, Alexander saying everything that was on his mind. Gage lowered his head to kiss me. He sighed against my mouth. "I love you so much."

"I love you, too. I love both of you."

"That's good." I could feel Alexander's smile through our link. "Because you're never getting rid of us."

Gage pushed inside of me. I cried out. It was so right having him there. A piece I'd been missing. I had to have this connection with him. How else to show him all the ways I loved him if not with my body? Words were never enough. Not for me, not for him. Not for any of us. What we did mattered, and I wanted to do this more than anything.

He pushed farther inside of me, and as I took him in, Alexander pressed closer against my rear. I could feel just how hard he was, too. Gage took no prisoners, he hardly left me time to breathe. His thrusts were strong and each one demanded my attention. I'd lose myself to the pleasure only to have it circle back again. Over and over. Why was this so amazing? How could I catch my breath? Did I want to? The questions came and went until there was nothing but their hands on my body and Gage's cock inside of me, pushing all my doubts away.

I came hard, and he followed me, shouting out my name.

I panted. I had to catch my breath, had to think, had to... only that wasn't happening. Alexander's mouth came down on mine. It was clearly his turn, and as much as I was sure I could object if I wanted to, I didn't have interest in stopping him. My ears rang.

How could there be so much pleasure? How could there be so much love? I shuddered as Gage pulled out of me, releasing me to Alexander. My Two was suddenly all over me. He gave me no space but then that was always Alexander. Whatever I needed, wherever I needed him, he was always there. He bit down on my neck, and I cried out, the pain bringing me back into the present.

I was fairly certain that had been his intention. I wrapped my legs tightly around him. He didn't get to dictate terms, and he knew it. He wanted me out of my head and in the moment? Great, he'd have me. But that meant I got to tell him what I desired, and what I needed right then was him inside of me. Not more foreplay. My body buzzed. Any more and it would be too much.

He got the hint, particularly because I held him still and wouldn't let him move other than where I wanted him. Alexander pressed himself at my entrance. I expected a fast push in but that wasn't what he did. Sometimes, Alexander really could surprise me. I forgot he had gentleness in him since he so rarely showed it.

But right then, tender was the only word I could think. He moved in and out of me with the utmost care. I clasped the side of his cheeks, watching his face. He was beautiful. Soon, he was so deep inside of me I would swear he could touch my soul. He held me close while he claimed me. I shattered around him, a long sigh escaping me as he filled the final cold spot of me. I warmed inside and even as that made happiness surge through me, it brought tears to my eyes.

How long could I have it? Was I to touch this kind of happiness for only just a second?

Alexander seemed to understand. His mouth met mine in the lightest of kisses. "Forever.

How did he know my unasked question? I shouldn't have been surprised. These guys were magic. They always had been. I'd just made myself forget so I could survive the separation.

I turned over to look at Gage. His eyes were closed. He was out cold. I guessed the co-joining had hit him.

I closed my eyes. The day ahead loomed like pain in this sweet moment. Alexander rolled me so I was on top of him and tucked me into the bed between Gage and him. I closed my eyes and listened to his heartbeat. I had to sleep. I'd never get through any of what was to come if I didn't.

❧

I WALKED THROUGH A LONG HALL, THE PURPLE RAYS OF THE sun hitting me through the floor to ceiling windows lining the walls. I kept my head down and walked forward. I didn't know where I was going just that I had to be there.

People passed me, everyone walking in the other direction. We were all training, all of us initiates preparing to battle in the war for humanity. I lifted my head to see if I knew anyone passing. At first I didn't, but then a face I recognized struck me so hard I stopped walking altogether.

It was Katrina. She was young, vibrant, happy. Her long black hair fell in waves down her back. Her face was makeup free. Nothing about her seemed stiff. She wasn't evil. Not yet.

She grabbed my arm, stopping to speak to me. "Aspen, are you okay?"

No, I wanted to say to her. No, I am absolutely not okay. Don't be this person. When they send you down, make different choices. Don't become the means to empower the Darkness. Stay as you are now. Don't do it, Katrina. Using your power, he gets so much stronger, and he starts Armageddon. But I didn't say any of that then so I couldn't say it in whatever this dream or memory was.

"I'm fine. Just thinking about the days ahead."

She leaned over to giggle in my ear. "Take one of your guys to bed. We can't do what we'll be able to do down below, but it's still fun."

I woke up slowly, the pseudo-memory not leaving me. Gage was still next to me, not moving in the utterly silent co-joining sleep. Alexander snored next to me, his hand on my back pressing me down into the mattress. Jamie sat on the end of the bed.

He lifted his eyebrows when it was clear I'd seen him. "You okay?"

"She's okay," Alexander spoke with his eyes closed. "She's wrapped up in me. Why wouldn't she be?"

"Well, because if you'd been awake you'd have felt through our link that she was distressed. I debated waking her, but then I thought maybe sleep was sleep." He rubbed my feet. "You okay, beautiful?"

I sat up. "I had a weird memory. I was talking to Katrina in the other place. Back before she was evil."

Alexander stretched, putting his arms over his head. "That would upset anyone."

The door creaked open and Reed stepped in, holding two cups of coffee. He handed one to both of us. "I hope this is okay. I've never actually made coffee before. I sort of trial and errored for a while. Then it occurred to me that I don't even know what good coffee tastes like or if either of you like it."

Jamie rose. "I don't like it. I prefer tea. Or maybe I just don't like Reed's coffee."

We were an odd bunch. I put my hand on Gage. He breathed. I just wanted to check. "Stone?"

"Still out. He's going to be pissed that Gage got to cuddle with you during his pass out time." Reed shook his head. "Hoping he's up soon since now we're facing the beginning of the end."

I sighed, rubbing my eyes before I took a sip of Reed's coffee. I actually loved coffee. And this was terrible. Reaching over Alexander, I set it down. He drank his like it was delicious. I was going to take over the coffee making, assuming we got to live long enough to have more.

I pulled my knees to my chest. "Seeing Katrina like that, it reminded me of before. She was kind. Super sweet. We weren't really friends, none of us were in that place, but we had each other's back. If the elders could see in the fate fountain what was going to happen, why send her to begin with? When you were all up there making decisions, Reed, why didn't you stop it? Send her to another time or make the decision not to send her at all?"

Reed sat down next to Jamie. "It doesn't work like that. They sent her down. She chose a path; that altered other paths. She didn't have to say yes to the Darkness, she could have said no and we'd be having a different conversation right now. The fact that these four were able to manipulate fate at all is impressive. There are a million small facts. Katrina chose. Should they have not allowed her to make the choice? That was above my power level."

"Then is my fate secured? What did the fountain say? Do I win or lose? In the one path you saw that led me here, did I win or lose today? You already know the outcome."

Reed shook his head. "I don't, actually. I was never part of this. I have no idea. Guys?"

Alexander leaned forward. "We don't know what happens next. Gage never saw past the part where we were able to get you powers. That was the goal. That was where we had screwed it up for you. You're supposed to be the Warrior."

I got out of the bed. "I'm the Warrior who had no training."

"Maybe that's better." Jamie's words startled me.

"How can that be?"

He pulled me to him. "You would have been at risk to be taken over by Katrina. Like any other Sister here. It was never guaranteed that Anne, Mika, Teagan, Beth—that any of them wouldn't go bad, so to speak. There are futures where that happened. They didn't. They made choices and that got them here. But we could all be done if Anne had succumbed. As it was, you were sort of protected. You had your memories. You were out of the fight. Somehow, none of your people were possessed in a world full of possession and you did learn to fight. Just your way. Not the traditional way."

"I..." I opened and shut my mouth. By divinity, he was right. I did have a tremendous amount of skills. I might be mediocre at demon killing but was the Darkness really a demon to begin with? He was something other. Beelzebub was a demon. He was helping to beat back this thing. The Darkness was something else. Like I was something else...

I rounded on Reed. "I don't think the best use of my time today is trying to get up to par to fight a battle we all know I can't win while down two guards. I think... I think I have to be me."

He smiled at me, slowly. "What do you have in mind?"

"I need to see Anne."

Alexander jumped up. "On it."

Maybe there was another way to beat him that had nothing to do with which one of us could dematerialize into cells and come out victorious. I knew the answer to that. He could. And there weren't enough years ahead of me in this nastiness to suddenly become the best fighter there ever was.

Alexander tore from the room, and I set about getting dressed. Someone had brought me some clothing, which meant I could change. I quickly bathed and put on the new outfit, which consisted of tight black pants and a white tunic that went down to my thighs. I could move in these. I'd never understood the traditional outfit that Katrina had the Sisters wear. How did they move in long skirts, heavy robes and veils?

There was one benefit to never having been in that Sisterhood. I didn't have to endure the wardrobe issues.

When I came out, Anne arrived, striding into the Sisterhood with her five guards behind her. I had the three of mine who were awake. The main room of the guesthouse would have been crowded, except someone had obviously designed this place with large meetings in mind. We all fit nicely.

"Alexander filled us in a little. You had a visit from the Darkness? He got through here? We have magical wards in place. That is unheard of. Other than Bob, we don't have demons here, and I'm fairly certain that demon could walk into the halls of divinity with no problems."

That was an image. The purple sun. Sister Superior. Bob. I shook my head, trying to clear my smile. This wasn't funny. Except it sort of was.

Anne smiled at me. Had she thought the same thing or was she just being kind to the woman who was supposed to save everyone? It didn't matter.

"Yes, he was here, and he says he'll kill a Sister every night if I don't meet him to fight."

She put her hands on her hips. "He must really be worried about you gaining strength."

"Perhaps. But I'm thinking that taking a crash course in demon killing is actually not the way to go. I was a strong fighter, but I don't think they chose me originally because of my kick butt fighting skills."

Now that I was saying all of this, I really had to hope I was right. I could be blowing this all to smithereens otherwise. There was more at stake than just my disappearing from existence. There was the entire future at risk.

She lifted her chin, turning slightly to look at Bryant. "We had a similar conversation this morning." He walked to her, taking her hand. "It's unreasonable to expect you to do this battle. I will do it. I'm Sister Superior. It's my job."

"Anne, you misunderstood me. I don't mean for someone else to fight it. I mean for me to fight it. But my way. With your help."

Bryant looked at Reed. He spoke to him. "What do you have in mind?"

The "not speaking to each other's Sister" thing was going to take some getting used to. I addressed him directly. "I mean I'm going to sneak attack him. But first I have to know who I'm dealing with. And for that I need your help. All of you. With your permission, Anne, I need to borrow Teagan and Mika. If they're willing. And then we have to figure out what to do about the threat of killing a Sister every night because this may take some time."

"I can help you with that," Krystal's voice boomed through the room.

Anne and I both jumped. Where had she come from? I realized the window in the side of the seating area was open. Krystal and her guys must have flown in.

Reed snorted. "There were some benefits to being able to fly and fit in small places."

"I still prefer the benefits to these forms." Stone appeared in the doorway. He leaned against the frame before making his way over to me. His white eyes fit in with the crowd. He kissed my shoulder before taking his place next to Alexander.

"Me, too," Reed agreed.

Krystal laughed. "Sorry. I think we might need to start

announcing ourselves better. All of that aside, I can help. You need to buy some time. Twenty-four hours at least. That means a Sister has to die." She raised her hand. "Signing up for the job. He can kill me."

My stomach clenched so hard it felt like someone had taken a knife and jabbed it into me. "You've died enough. No one is dying. There has to be a way to... I don't know... avoid that."

"You're right. I'm not dying. I'm already dead. Sort of." She winked at Titus. "The point is he can think he killed me. He doesn't know what happened to me other than I took care of Katrina. So let's just let him think he did, shall we? We can pull that off for one day. Can you get yourself started on whatever you need in that much time?"

I nodded. "I hope so."

"Good enough. That's all we can do, right? You're all of our last hope. So we put our faith in you."

If I was making a huge mistake it was only twenty-four hours and no one would get hurt.

Anne put her hands in mine. "What do you need?"

"I think to start, I need Teagan."

When I'd wanted to break into the Sisterhood, I'd listened in the brothels to stories the men would tell about Katrina. Rumors about her. Sometimes gossip was just that and worthless of inquiry. Sometimes there was truth in the tale. I'd figured out she was vain and sure of herself. She didn't expect anyone to break in. She was more concerned with her Sisters trying to get out. Katrina didn't care about the non-Sisters who made things run and work for her. I'd just pretended to be one.

Anne nodded. "I'll go see if she's up, and if she's not, I'll get her up. Krystal, what do you need?"

"Shut down the Sisterhood like you're on high alert. Increase the wards. Tell Daniella they're just not strong enough. And good luck. I still have this sense of cyclical in my mind. I can't let it go."

"Then don't. That's how divinity speaks to us in that role you're playing. An incessant chattering. It must matter. We just don't know how yet." Reed addressed Krystal directly. My guys had apparently not gotten the message that they couldn't speak to the Sisters. Or maybe it was just Reed. He'd been talking to them all for years. Old habits died hard.

Krystal nodded. "I'll be there tonight. Playing the role of a lifetime. Don't believe it when I look dead. Or fake like you believe it. We're doing this thing."

I felt the absence of Gage move through me. He'd be pivotal in this pursuit. He could see things laid out so clearly. I looked for him in our link. He was there, just sleeping. I let him rest. I wasn't even certain I could rouse him if I wanted to but I wasn't going to risk it. Whatever happened to them with co-joining they needed sound sleep after and divinity saw that they got it.

I followed Anne outside, waiting in the courtyard. It was a dusty day. The amount of dirt in the air made it hard to tell exactly how the weather was. I coughed into my hand and then cleared my throat. Krystal had saved the planet, but if we didn't get this under control soon, it was all going to go to hell again.

"Hello, dear." Daniella caught my attention. "Okay if I observe? Anne says you have something to try. Sometimes I can help with things. I've been around a long time."

She had the kindest eyes. Not to mention they were in color. "How did you get your color back? Why aren't you white?"

"It's a trick. When your last one wakes up you can do it. Takes a full co-joining. I have lots of small things I can teach you. Oh, I'm not powerful like the four of you are, but I have life experience."

I squeezed her fingers. "I think you may be the most powerful of any of us. You left early. You must have. That was brave. Took your men and made a life. That's... energy. That's fluidity. That's taking control of your own destiny. I think you're probably the bravest of any of us."

She blinked tears away. "Oh no, dear. I think you are."

Teagan hurried toward me. Her guards were right behind her. She stopped in front of Daniella and me. "How can I help?"

Anne ran up a second later. I guessed I was going to do this with an audience. "How far back can you see?" I addressed Teagan.

"I don't know, actually. I don't generally control the visions. I go back as far as I need them to go back."

I could understand that. I wasn't sure I was in control of any of this. I was certainly trying to be, and I imagined she was as well. "Can you see the other place?"

"Sometimes. Not often."

That was interesting. "I see it in my memory all the time."

Teagan lifted her eyebrows slowly. "All the time?"

"I do. I'm wondering if you could try—and if you can't do it we'll work something else out—if you could try to see the Darkness as he was before. I need to know who he is. I want to understand him. Not excuse him, per se." I didn't know why I felt like I had to add that part but I did. "I need to see who he was. So we can work on figuring out where he is spending his time. I want to catch him by surprise. On my terms, not his."

She bit down on her lip. "I don't know if I can."

"You can," Reed spit out and then winced. "Sorry. Thaddeus, would it be okay if I spoke to Teagan?"

Her one-eyed guard stared at Reed for a second. "When this is over you and I are going to spar with swords."

Reed rolled his eyes. "Fine. We'll see who has a bigger

penis later. For now can we stay focused? You had your run at this. You did a great job playing your role. My turn."

"Talk to her sparingly."

Reed nodded. "I'll try to minimize my words." Reed approached Teagan. "You are so loaded with powers, Sister Teagan, that they flow through you faster than you can even process them. Your gifts are immense. Let's figure out how to get the memories she needs."

Teagan's gaze didn't leave me. "When memories move through me they don't stay very long. I can hardly hold onto them. They're like fleeting visions. Aspen, it sounds like you hold onto things longer."

"I never lost my memory. That might be the difference."

Teagan turned to her guards. What was she doing? For a second, she stared at all of them as though they silently communicated. Were they? Or did they just understand each other so well that sometimes verbal communication wasn't necessary. Finally, she turned back to me.

"Yesterday you asked Daniella about power. She told you that power goes to the person as they need it. That everyone absorbs power the way they are supposed to. That's right, Sister Daniella?"

The older sister nodded. "Absolutely correct."

"Then I give you mine, Aspen. Take it. Beat this man."

Wait. What? I shouted a no a second before Teagan's power blasted into me like a bomb going off in my head. I lost consciousness, and the world became nothing.

❧ 10 ❧

I woke up in a daze, the world spinning. Stone had his arms around me as he muttered something soothing in my ear. I had a hard time making out the words. Teagan was gone and so were her guards. Daniella screamed, her mouth covered by her hands like she wanted to stop herself.

My hands shook. Clearly, not much time had passed. "Why did she do that?"

"Because she wanted you to be able to do what you needed to do." Reed pounded on the ground. "She could have killed you."

That was his biggest concern? That she could have killed me? "Where is she?"

"She vanished." Jamie was bent over, his hands on his knees.

"They're all gone. The children, too." Bryant was out of breath. He must have run somewhere and then come back. "Like she was never here at all."

Anne was silent and still, like a statue of herself.

"I didn't mean for this." I needed her to understand. "It's not my intention to destroy Sisters."

117

I looked at the sky. Krystal had become a bird. Was Teagan? I didn't see anyone up there, not a single raven. Did that mean that was all wrong or just the end of something?

Anne touched my shoulder. "I know you didn't. And I don't think Teagan was wrong. She's impulsive but rarely out of touch." Anne sighed. "Let's not waste this with thinking about what if. She's my best friend. I will miss her every second until I can see her again, but I will see her. After we win. You have her powers. You can hold onto old memories. Find him."

I wanted to sleep for a year. I wanted to cry. I doubted my legs would work but none of that mattered in the least. I had a task to accomplish, I was going to get it done.

Of course, I had no idea how to use Teagan's powers or if they would even work that way for me. I turned to Daniella, who had finally stopped screaming. "Help me."

She nodded once. "I will. Give me your hands." I put mine in hers. Warmth moved through me. I'd never asked Daniella exactly what she could do to assist me and yet I'd known she could. Was this because Teagan had known? How much of herself had Teagan given to me?

Daniella held my gaze. "We just have to wake up the part you need. Ah, yes, it's right there behind your left eye. I can see it."

A prick of pain startled me, and I blinked to clear it. As I did, the world shifted. Yes, I could see the past if I wanted to. If I looked at Daniella's One right now, I'd know his whole story. But I didn't want to do that. No, not at all. I had a task. A solo one and unless learning the past out of every person here would help me I wasn't going to do it.

Instead, I pictured the figure that came to me in my dream, the monster that climbed onto my wall. I had Krystal's powers, not her memory but in the same way that I had known Teagan would turn to Daniella, I knew how Krystal felt about the Darkness. I could *feel* it. The terror he'd given her, the way he made her skin crawl.

And it was enough. I didn't need him to be present. I could see him.

I followed his trail. I didn't want to see him alone. I grabbed onto Stone tighter. "Go with me."

"Wherever you go, I go."

And just like that we were somewhere else. I looked up at Stone and he back at me. "This is a vision. The Darkness' past. Whatever he was. Whoever he was."

Stone nodded. "A vision. We're not really here."

"No, we have to watch." I steeled my shoulders. "This is what I needed to do. This is why Teagan did what she did." I couldn't stand that thought. "I wish she hadn't. I mean, did she wake up this morning and think 'I'm going to sacrifice myself and my whole family today?' "

Stone kissed my forehead. "Don't turn this into your fault. People make decisions. I don't think she made it alone either. They were all in on it. Let's not dwell on what was. Why are we here?"

He was right. Stone was always great at keeping me on task. We moved forward. We'd been brought here to see what the Darkness' past was. I hoped I wasn't about to walk in on him as an infant. That wasn't going to be particularly useful. Unless this whole thing was being caused by some sort of mommy issues.

The scene shifted around us like the past was catching up to us. I didn't understand this. Was this what Teagan's life had been like? Constant movements of visions? We stood in a bar.

A redheaded man stood on top of a table, yelling at the top of his lungs. "And I told you people what would happen if you didn't pay us to take care of you? We're going to let the demons eat you alive. Is that what you wanted? To be eaten alive?"

His voice was jarring, I'd heard it twice when it was connected to a shapeless body. Now to see him looking human? It made my skin crawl. He wasn't a handsome man. Maybe that wasn't nice to say. But I really didn't think the figure of the future Darkness was all that handsome. And that's all there was to it.

His hair was bright red. Although none of my guys were redheads, some of the other guards were. They could be quite handsome. So it wasn't the hair that set me off. He had blue eyes and his face was long. I think it had to be the sheer negative energy coming off of him. I was readily of the opinion that how a person acted could actually alter how I felt about them physically.

"I want the money, and I want it now."

He couldn't see us. He was just human and this was a visit to the past. To something that had happened already.

Stone shook his head. "Shit."

"What?" I looked over at my guy. He couldn't be resonating more different energy if he tried. He was pure love. His strong features were beautiful.

"Aspen, look at his outfit. He's a guard."

I gasped. No one turned to look at us. We were outsiders on this memory.

"He's a guard, and he's threatening these people with demonic interference. Killing them. Eating them." I didn't actually think demons ate people. They possessed them, sucked them dry of energy. Maybe it was the same thing—but chewing down? That wasn't one of the things demons did. I didn't think.

Not that it mattered. The fact that he threatened them was enough. They didn't know what demons could and couldn't do.

He did.

"How is this...?" Guards didn't do this. Oh, who was I

kidding? Katrina had been a Sister and look what she did. We all knew by now that those who shouldn't do bad things were often the worst offenders. "Did you know him? Up there? Is it possible he has stolen the clothes?"

I hated the idea of a guard betraying the world. Sisters were one thing. I could almost understand how some of us went bad. Power was maddening. But my guards were loyal even when all hope had been lost. That was more common. They found us. They searched and never stopped, even when they didn't know what they were looking for. Mika's guys had found her when they hadn't known they were guards.

What in the hell was this?

"I don't remember him, but we really mostly stuck to ourselves and stalked you until we could have you. I mean, I knew the big ones. Bryant. Thaddeus. Titus. Neil. Carrie. Those people. I knew of them. I was never One and that meant I only had to deal so far with those outside of my group. I liked it better that way. This guy? No, I have no recollection of him."

The memory shifted. We were outside. He was with four other guys, all of them dressed as guards. He held gold up in his hands.

"I told you. I told you that we'd earn more this time."

One of the others shook his head rapidly. "I can't do this anymore. This isn't right. This isn't what we're supposed to be doing, and she wouldn't like it."

"I'm so sick of her. Why do we have to do what she says all the time? Who died and made her in charge anyway? She's only a mid-level sister fighting nothing demons."

I whirled around to look at this scene even as I listened to them bicker. Everything was green and lush. Carts were pulled by us, people looked healthy. Whatever demons that were here that the Sister this man didn't love fought were probably never more than mid-level. The world had always had mid-level demons. It wasn't until the Darkness brought out the big guns that the apocalypse started and we found ourselves in this mess. This was how things were supposed to look.

"They're breaking up. And it's not just that they're really angry. They're ending. I've never seen a guard group do this before. Even when Reed became Brother Raven, we never wanted to be entirely done with him. These guys are done with him."

One of the others was yelling now. "Take your gold, and I hope that you choke on it."

The redheaded Darkness surged forward, drawing his sword. Soon they were all fighting on the street, Darkness in the center. I had nothing else to call him. No one had used his name. That was okay. I knew I'd be good without ever knowing it.

"Stop." A brown haired woman ran toward them. Her eyes were Sister white. I didn't know her any more than Stone knew the Darkness. It didn't matter. "Stop, please. I love you all."

The Darkness swung around, stabbing her right in the stomach. Her mouth fell open, a kind of guttural sound releasing from her as she seemed to choke on the moment. I grabbed onto Stone as horror rushed through me.

The other men were around her, grabbing the sword, talking to her, and in the way that some things are clear because they are, I knew they'd never be able to save her. She was dead. He'd killed her. I forced my attention off the blonde woman's face and back to the Darkness.

I saw nothing there. Not shock. Not remorse. Nothing at all.

He wasn't the least bit sorry.

We were jolted back into our bodies, and I put my head between my knees in order to try not to vomit. It wasn't the memory traveling that bothered me but the scene we'd witnessed. "Anything you've ever heard about the Darkness is a lie."

Anne bent over to speak to me. "What do you mean?"

"I always heard the rumors: that this happened because he was somehow screwed over by a woman. Not true. He was a guard, and he killed his Sister. He was malicious, unfeeling. I've never seen anything quite like it before."

She covered her mouth. "Who is the Sister?"

"I don't know her, and Stone didn't know him."

Here we were in Anne's Sisterhood. The Prophet and the Healer had given me their powers. I was supposed to be the Warrior. Anne was Sister Superior down here on the planet and somewhere nearby Mika was the Oracle.

We had titles like they were supposed to make us important. But this whole thing had been caused by people whose names we didn't know. What happened to him? He died as humans did. He was either killed right then or later. In any case, he was sent to where those souls who were unredeemable went.

But this guy had come back, and he'd brought Hell with him.

I supposed at this point names didn't matter. The question was why divinity let it happen. Oh, I didn't need an answer. I knew what they'd tell me. Choice. It was always choice. We could drown in our decision-making, we were free to do everything wrong. We were totally within our rights to bring on the apocalypse, and they couldn't do anything but send me down here and hope that my choices meant I'd deal with it appropriately.

"It's a big deal." Stone kissed my head. "I think we were hoping to have some sort of answer as motive. Something she could use against him. Or some sense of where he is. We got none of that. Just an unwell person who was murderous in life and is now murderous in death. It is really going to come down to a battle." Stone sighed, rubbing his face. "It's bad."

Anne nodded. "I see." She took Bryant's hand. "Well, we still have Krystal tonight, buying us some time. Let's reconvene in the evening and see what we think then."

"If I have to fight, shouldn't I be training?" Not that I particularly felt up to that. I didn't in the slightest. Just the opposite.

Anne hugged me to her. "I think your earlier point stands. You can't learn everything we know in an afternoon. You've bested two demons. I think you can fight just as you need to."

She did? Why was her voice shaking?

"Anne?"

She took two steps away from me. "See you tonight."

Sister Superior starting to cry? That had to mean she thought all hope was lost. The crowd around us thinned until it was just my guys with me alone in the courtyard. "I'd really started to believe that maybe I could do it."

Reed picked me up into his arms. "I still think you can. I just think it's going to be complicated. No sense at all where he might be?"

"All we saw was bar and outside the bar. I don't think the Darkness can be frequenting pubs, can he?"

Alexander shook his head. "He's in a body of some kind. He had to have taken one over after Katrina left him. I guess that body could be drinking. Should we go check the pub?"

Stone shook his head. "He went to the pub to extort money. I don't think he requires that either. No, I have no idea what we should do."

Jamie hadn't moved. "What do you want to do, Aspen? You're the one with the powers. Do you want to fight? Train? We'll do that. Do you want to go back to the guesthouse and sleep? We'll do that. You tell me."

The decision was made for me. One second I stared at

him, the next the weight of Teagan's powers rushed through me and the world went black.

✦

I STOOD IN THE CENTER OF A CIRCLE. WHAT IN THE WORLD had happened? The sounds of drums in the distance filled my ears. I turned around. My guys were there with me, frozen like statues, with masks over their faces. I rushed toward them. What had happened? What was this?

"Reed?" I pulled on his body, but he didn't move. His eyes stared far away as though he couldn't see me. The same happened with all five of them.

Sweat broke out on my body. Something was wrong. The last thing I could remember was Jamie asking me what I wanted to do. What had happened? By divinity, what was this place?

"Aspen." Daniella limped to me. "It's okay. This is... where we are spiritually while we are down there fighting. Look up. You'll see old friends."

I lifted my head to where she indicated to see dancing birds in the sky. No, that wasn't what they were. "The spirits. The ones who watch us." Sister Superior herself might be dancing in the sky. The real one, not Anne, her voice.

Daniella nodded. "Yes, dear. They watch us. And your guards... they're not fully made of metal. They're almost ready to break free. You've entirely co-joined. That's good. It went fast. The spirits were wary that you might take too long to forgive. But you didn't. You are beyond worthy of what will happen to you next.

Her words stuttered my heart. "What will happen?"

"That's not for me to say. As you've been struggling with, it's always about choice isn't it, and you have some more to do. I would have liked to have known you better."

I swallowed through the pain her words caused. Choice. Choice. Choice. I didn't want to make any more. But I supposed sometimes there was no alternative. Pick a path, walk it. Live with the consequences, hope you're correct.

"Is Teagan okay? I hate what she did."

Daniella did answer for a second. "She placed a lot of trust in you, in the people who chose you, and I suppose the answer to your question is that we don't yet know. Teagan sees the world differently—based on her powers. She saw something in you. I trust Teagan. Even when she screws up, she fixes it. She wouldn't have done that without reason." Daniella touched my long dark hair. "Good luck. Darkness to light. I finally understand."

I HATED PASSING OUT. I WAS SUPPOSED TO BE TOUGH. Fainting didn't seem like it fit into that image. I woke up stretched over Gage. The room was quiet, but in the hallway, I could hear voices. Reed. Alexander. Jamie. They weren't fighting, I could tell by their tone. One of them laughed. That was a good sound.

If I was about to die in the next twenty-four hours I wanted to slip from the universe hearing that sound. Their happiness was everything.

Gage stretched, and I lifted my head to regard him. "You're awake."

"For a bit now. The guys filled me in." A surge of pleasure moved through me. They were all in my mind now. That was what I'd needed. A complete co-joining. I had it. I could feel them all like a joyous rush of fullness I'd never had before.

I snuggled down into Gage's side. "I think I had weird dreams."

"Oh yes? What about?"

"You guys were statutes."

He was silent. "Really? I feel like I've had that dream myself. Stuck as a statue... can't really see."

I sat up straight. "Well, I don't like that at all."

"Me either."

A knock sounded and Jamie poked his head in. "Sweetheart, we better go if we're going to try to watch whatever Krystal is going to do now."

I nodded. That made sense. I'd really slept a long time. "We both had a weird dream about statues."

Jamie furrowed his brow. "Me, too."

Okay, this was very bad news. What did any of it mean? I needed to find Daniella as soon as this part was over and get some answers. If they were all having the dream, then maybe it wasn't a dream. I got out of bed fast. I was still dressed, which made things easier, but my head didn't feel like it was on straight.

Teagan's powers came with a darkness attached to them. It wrapped around me like a lasso. How did I know it was Teagan's? Somehow it tasted like her. Krystal's were someone flavored like Krystal. I didn't have any of my own, so it felt as though my cells were constantly ingesting other people's stuff.

I shook my head. This was fine. I would make this work. I would beat the Darkness, somehow. I would... find out why I saw in black and white when I battled, if that mattered. I would bring back Teagan and her family.

I would be better than I'd ever been.

The weight of this pressed on my shoulders. Jamie and Gage moved to stand next to me. Of course they would know, they'd be able to feel the stress through our link. Jamie tugged me to him. "We don't have to watch."

"Yes, we do. Even when things are hard, we do them. Sometimes we do them because they're hard."

"ARE YOU TALKING TO US OR TO YOURSELF?" GAGE HAD A way of putting things that cut to the chase.

I side-eyed him. "Maybe both."

"Fair enough."

❦

REED

I'D KNOWN ALL DAY SOMETHING BAD WAS GOING TO happen. I'd woken with the feeling, and it hadn't passed. When Aspen had fainted, I'd thought for sure that was it, the bad thing. But the sensation was still there. I stared up at the sky. Not a single raven to be seen.

That wasn't good news.

I stepped out of the cabin, letting Aspen dart ahead of me. She was the Sister. That was how it worked. But I kept pace. She wouldn't get too far ahead of me, not ever. I'd take down any threats that came to her.

Where were the other Sisters? Didn't anyone else want to watch whatever Krystal was going to do?

The sun started to set in the sky, and in the distance, I could hear noises, shouts, moans, and hisses. The Darkness was putting on a show. He must be pissed as hell that my Sister didn't show up to fight him. He wanted to beat her while she was weak.

But that was the problem. We couldn't get her strong. I saw it on Anne's face today. She didn't think we could do what we needed to, and Aspen was lost to the stress of it.

We came to a stop by the gate, and I nudged her with my shoulder. "Nothing bad is going to happen tonight."

"You can't promise me that."

She was right. "No, but words have power. Saying it aloud might make that happen."

Aspen side-eyed me in the way no one else ever could. My love just had a special knack to it. I'd missed it in the endless years away from her. "You think something bad is going to happen. I can feel it in our link."

"Yes, but I have hope that it won't."

A bang sounded, and the ground shook. I steadied myself. Whatever Krystal had done, it was over. Now we waited.

There really wasn't anything else to do.

I took Aspen's hands in mine, and I linked our fingers. She was mine. Whatever the outcome.

�֍ I I ֍

ASPEN

Krystal flew through the gate, a black raven with a blonde feather before she landed, five black birds around her. She shifted, which never ceased to amaze me, then strode toward me with a fast gait.

"Well, that is done. He thinks he killed me." She shrugged. "Great. The guys did a great performance of mourning me. When he tried to get through Daniella's wards this time, he failed. I hope I bought you time. That's what I think you need. Time."

I nodded at her. "I don't know how I can thank you."

"You can beat him tomorrow."

That seemed awfully fast. "Tomorrow?"

She nodded. "If things are going to go as I imagine they will, then yes it will be tomorrow." She stared at me a second. "I don't really understand why they made you do this with so much doubt. I think surely it would have been better for you to believe in yourself fully. But then again, I don't know what it really will take to beat him. Maybe if you started with a full tank it wouldn't work. Or..." She looked away. "Maybe it takes someone who lived as a human. I bet that's it. I wish they would tell me. I'd break rules and tell you."

Reed laughed. "They never do tell you anything that can really help."

Krystal touched Reed's arm. "You helped. You brought them to me. I'll never forget that." She stepped back from me. I noted that her guards didn't freak out that she'd touched and spoken to Reed. Maybe they didn't have the same issues the ones here had. Maybe it had to do with being technically dead.

"Thank you to the rest of you for all you did so we could get to this path." She nodded at my guards. "Any other situation and we'd never even have a chance. I know you had your selfish reasons, but they turned out to be the right ones."

"Sounds like you're leaving." Gage spoke from behind me on the left.

Krystal nodded. "I've interfered as much as I can. I'm getting signaled. You have things to do, and it's time for me to leave. I hope I see you again, Aspen."

"Because if I lose, I vanish, never to be seen again." I hated it, but saying hard things aloud didn't make them any less hard. I couldn't live in denial.

She did me the favor of not denying it either. "Good luck."

"Krystal." I grabbed her arm. "Before you go, is there anything you can tell me? Anything at all?"

Surely, there had to be something else. Or maybe I was grasping at straws. She stared into my eyes. "The path went askew so many times. People didn't do what they should have. Katrina? No one saw that. A small nothing path that should never have happened. You? Your guys only think it was a minuscule possibility. You are exactly who you should be. They are certain of that. You are exactly what they wanted. When the time comes, you are what was needed. I can't explain it because I can't see it other than that. A sense from them. You brought... hope. He's redheaded." He must want his original look again.

I didn't know if that helped anything, but I didn't suppose I could ask her for anything more. "Thank you, Krystal."

"Goodbye, Sister." She took off to the sky, taking her five guys with her until they all seemed to vanish into the clouds.

"You always brought me hope." I turned as Alexander spoke. I wouldn't have expected him to say something so sentimental. I waited for the punch line and when nothing came, I had to swallow the tears that threatened.

When I could, I finally spoke. "Why?"

He didn't flinch or look away. "Because you existed to begin with. That meant there was a reason for everything." He took my hand and placed it over his heart. "I can feel it. Here."

"Aspen," Anne's voice called out into the night. While we'd stood talking, the sun had gone to bed. I hoped it would actually come back tomorrow.

I shivered. My mother would have said it felt like someone walked on my grave.

Anne held out her hand. "Could you come? We're waiting for you between the main house and the guesthouse."

I kept my back straight. She wasn't my enemy. I knew that in my soul. Right then, however, I wasn't certain that she was my friend either. We didn't really know each other. If I wanted to I could look through Anne's entire past. But I didn't think I had that kind of time.

I walked forward. "Anne, I feel like I'm not heading for good news. Are you going to string me up by my fingernails?"

She didn't laugh. That wasn't a good sign. It had been a pretty good joke. It at least deserved a smile, which I wasn't getting.

Reed must have agreed with me. He put his hand out in

front of me to stop me from walking. "Demons I'll never hold you back from. This I don't like. What is she going to do?"

Bryant answered him. "Anne would never hurt her. We're going to help her embrace her destiny."

"That's not an answer."

Instead of me walking forward, the entire Sisterhood seemed to turn the corner and walk toward me. Anne sighed. "This was going to be hard. Once I understood what had to happen it was always going to be hard."

"What is happening?" Gage moved into formation. Were we going to battle? "Because if I need to hurt all of you to keep her safe, I will."

"Of that we have no doubt," Neil, Mika's One answered. "We'd all do that. It makes it so much harder that the right thing to do might cause our loves pain."

"Enough with the nonsense." Alexander's annoyance charged through our link. All five of my guys were over this experience. Maybe disappearing to the beach was actually the way to go.

Mika walked toward me. "I missed what happened with Teagan. But I heard after the fact that the Darkness is a former guard who betrayed his Sister. Is that right?"

She took my hand in hers. I felt no malice from her and shook my head to stop Jamie when he would have removed her hand from mine. No wonder the guards got so funny around here about people touching each other or even talking. Not trusting motive was a problem. When had they all stopped just saying what they meant? Was this a leftover problem from when Katrina was in charge? Protect yourself or risk yourself?

In that moment, I could feel Mika's sorrow pressing at me. "That's right. What's wrong?"

"I'm sorry you have to fight him. That this job falls to you. I've been upset at times over my own role in this. It's not fun to see where the initiates are being born, to be responsible for the threads of the future. There were times Katrina could see through my eyes. I understand now how that happened. It wasn't her, it was him. I'm connected to all of us in this fight. He's a guard. That makes me linked to him. He used that."

Her powers didn't seem like any fun at all. "You didn't separate families. That was the big thing. The public knew that. You let the families keep the babies until they were older, and you didn't ask them to come here away from their loved ones."

"Well, I tried." She hugged me. "You need to find him when he doesn't expect it. Teagan could narrow her focus. I never could. But the two powers together? Yes, they'll do that for you. Try looking through his eyes?"

I should have known what she was going to do but I didn't. A surge of heat hit me before Mika's powers transferred over to me. My knees gave way, and I cried out.

"I don't want this." I yelled to the gathered crowd. "I don't want you to leave. I don't want you to do this."

"That's unfortunate." Daniella strode toward me. "Because what we all realized is the way we could help you was to give you us. You can't learn it. You can have it. All of it."

Reed growled, a noise I'd never heard him make before. "She can't handle that much power."

"She can. I enhance power. It's one of the things I do."

Daniella. Beth. It was a wave of power as one-by-one, they hit me.

There was nothing my guards could do. Their frustration surged through the link. After Mika, the Sisters weren't even touching me as they ended their own existence and gave over their powers. Reed continued to try, to plead with them to stop.

"Anne, they're going to kill her. No one can take this much power. You're destroying her."

Were they? I wasn't feeling anything. The world whited out little by little until all color started to vanish from my view. This wasn't the same as my black and white fighting, this was... leaving. They wanted to help me, but they really were killing me.

"She won't die." Anne had tears in her voice. I couldn't see her, but I could hear it. "See, I have very few gifts to actually give you, Aspen. The others were more powerful than me in a lot of ways. But Divinity did give me one thing I could do that no one else can. I can bring back life. You won't lose yours. Your life is mine to give you. I hope you gentleman will excuse the touching. This is how I can do this. I didn't know you, Aspen. I know that I love you. Sister to Sister. First to Last."

Her mouth met mine. It wasn't a press of a kiss, not a sexual embrace. It was more, tender, like a mother might kiss a child. She tasted like strawberries. That fact was bizarre in the mix of all the other things going on. But as suddenly as she kissed me, the world came back into view. For maybe half a minute, we stood there before she vanished, my life suddenly back in full force.

My ears rang, and my heart raced.

I was all alone save my guys. The courtyard was empty. I waited to pass out, but the unconsciousness never came. Instead, I was charged beyond belief. I could probably climb the side of the house if I wanted to.

Tears leaked from my eyes. As much as I could take on the world, I was utterly overwhelmed. What was I supposed to do with this?

Jamie knelt down in front of me. He was pale. I'd never seen him so visibly shaken before. "Aspen?"

"I'm alive."

He nodded. "Good. Let's start with that. Are you okay?"

"No. How could I be?" I struggled to my feet. Were my legs going to quit working again? My cells digested the magic, the sheer power. There was no pain. Not like the first time. Daniella had seen to that. I could feel her, taste her on my tongue as thoroughly as I could Anne. What she knew existed inside of me.

Stone threw his hands in the air. "They didn't ask you if you wanted this."

"Because they knew I'd say no. Not a single one of them would have signed up for this mess. But they saw no other way. And this isn't a democracy. Anne says what happens."

Reed was silent but only because he fumed. He'd helped all these people find their soul mates and they'd turned around and hurt me. Funny, I could read my guys almost completely through the link with the power increase. Would that have happened over time?

I'd never know.

"Are you guys up for a little fighting? This happened. Let's see what I can do with it." I took a deep breath, relaxing my neck muscles.

A muscle ticked in Reed's jaw. "You want to kill some demons?"

"Yes."

He nodded once. "Let's do it."

I could see Daniella's wards as though they were living, breathing organisms surrounding the Sisterhood. Like living spider webs minus the spider. I lifted my finger, spinning it around until the webs vanished.

The demons hadn't been able to get through them. Now they could.

I walked to the gates and swung them open. I couldn't be more obvious than that. This Sisterhood was open for business. The demons should come and get me. Not to mention,

I was going to be a walking, talking demon magnet. Teagan hadn't been able to keep them away from her and now neither could I.

The Sisters risked everything for me. They'd traded their lives and put the existence of their children on the line with the idea that I could do this. I hated it. I didn't want this responsibility. I supposed I'd always had it even if I hadn't known it.

The Warrior had to kill the Darkness for all humanity to continue. The concept was better than the reality.

"Why did I want this so much?" I asked no one in particular. "I spent twenty-four years bitter and angry that it was taken away from me."

Gage stood next to me. "Is this a case of be careful what you wish for?"

"Yes. Or divine manipulation. Maybe they needed to see just how much I wanted it. When this is over, I'm no one's pawn ever again."

He kissed my cheek. "You aren't now. I'd wager you could take on divinity itself if you wanted to."

My powers surged to life as a type two demon appeared at my gate. He was some kind of incubus. I twisted my wrist, and he exploded. My powers had barely turned on and that had taken no time at all. Which Sister knew how to do that? I could feel her, but I didn't even know her name.

Like the one the Darkness had killed...

"That was too easy. I need another one."

I hadn't even broken out in a sweat, and my vision remained colorful. Was it going to from now on? There was no one left to ask.

ALEXANDER

I STOOD BACK AND WATCHED MY GIRL TAKE OUT DEMON after demon that came to the gate as though they were bugs she squashed under her feet. She was bored, and I was holding back my terror from our link. If she looked, she'd see mild amusement from me. I looked at Reed. If his link was to be believed, he was in the same zone as me.

I'd bet gold he was also terrified. It wasn't our role to let her know when we were scared, it was up to us to help her when she was. The problem? Aspen had always walked around with a drop of anxiety. That was part of who she was, it was her nature to worry. And she wasn't. She was angry; I could feel that from her and divinity knew she was entitled to be pissed off at all of the things that had been done to her, but the worry was gone.

Had she just decided that what would be would be or was this more concerning? Did all of the power she received take away what was at its root the heart of Aspen—her ability to feel? Right now not only did she have no fear—something that seemed a very good idea when battling even the smallest of demons since Sisters died all the time in minor demon attacks—but the only thing I was getting from her was annoyance.

I wasn't going to lose the heart of my girl to this mess. Fuck the universe. She was all that mattered. I'd signed on to help the cause, my early born soul feeling a calling that I answered. I'd stayed because of her. It wasn't that I didn't give a shit about humanity. Of course, I did. At the heart of it, what was the point of living without love? What was the point of every day if we didn't have that? I did. And I'd guard and protect her while she lived out her role even from herself.

Reed was her One. That meant certain things weren't

going to happen from him. We all had our mission. From this point on, Aspen's heart and soul was mine.

I took her hand. "Hey, want to eat something?"

She stopped staring at the gate and turned to me. By divinity, those eyes. They could wound. They could scorch. They could heal. I'd drown in them. I wanted them to be the last thing I saw when I slipped from this place to whatever came next.

I wanted them to never lose the essential soul that was Aspen.

She shook her head. "I'm not hungry at all. Right now, I feel like I never need to eat again."

"Well, that's not good," Gage spoke from my left. He was right. It wasn't at all okay. I'd try again.

"Take a break, Aspen. Please. Let's process what happened here."

Just then the house shook. We all whirled around to see the Sisterhood crumble to the ground, the demon Bob—also known as Beelzebub—rising from beneath it. They'd had to rebuild this place multiple times from what I'd heard thanks to the coming and going of that guy.

Her powers shot to life, and she breathed in hard. There was her anxiety. That was a good sign. There were still some things that could make Aspen scared. I didn't want her fearful, but we lived and died sometimes because we listened to our fear.

She needed it. My woman was still in there even mixed in with all the other Sisters who were taking space that didn't belong to them.

ASPEN

I stared up at the demon the others called Bob—that I would never disrespect with that kind of nickname—and tried not to shake where I stood. I didn't know what kind of arrangement Anne had with him, but she was gone now. It was just me.

"You want to fight me? With all your new powers?"

I clamped down on my nerves. I didn't know if they were making me sharper or sloppy. "I don't know. I'm here to kill demons."

"You're here to kill a human. A man who fell so far from the light he can't see it anymore. Stop wasting your time on nothingness, disturbing my sleep, and proving yourself to not be the woman you need to be." He flicked his finger, and I shot backward, slamming into Gage's chest.

He caught me and set me down, gently on my feet. "You okay?"

"He's made his point." I pointed at Beelzebub. "How about you? Want to give me all of your powers to take on the Darkness?" I strode toward him. "Any words of wisdom to relay?"

He laughed, throwing his head back. "Don't die, little Sister. Or if you do, try to do it quietly. I'm tired of all this noise. I'm going to feed. Be done when I get back."

I almost argued with him about calling me little but somehow I managed to keep my mouth shut. It was clear the demon could kill me, and I didn't know how that worked in terms of beating the Darkness. Was he easier or harder to manage than Beelzebub?

He turned toward me one last time before he spoke again. "Keep in mind, he isn't a demon. He's managed to convince demons to follow him who would better have stayed where they were. He's a human. You aren't killing a demon. You're killing an evil human. I will manage the demons left here, assuming you can actually do this. If you can't... well, all good things must come to an end. Evil things are different."

Jamie put his hand on my arm. "Are you okay? That was quite a fall you took."

I had to pull my attention from the exiting demon. I swung around to regard my guards. "Maybe it's Gage we should worry about. He was the one who caught me."

His smile was swift, kind, in the way Gage always was. "You're nothing to catch. Jamie and I could toss you about and never get tired."

I wagged my finger at him. "One does not go around tossing a Sister, and I might be small, but I think at this point it's safe to say that I could kick butt if I wanted to."

Gage threw his head back, laughing. "Of that I never had any doubt."

"It's time to see where he is." I steeled my back. "I feel like there is a clock ticking in my head. It might be my imagination but the feeling is the same. I need to hurry. If none of this is accidental then..."

Reed finished my words. "Then there is no time to waste. I understand the feeling. But you aren't doing this alone." He extended his hand. "I'm with you. Take me on the journey."

I'd be glad for the company. In the end, I was going to do what had to be done alone. Then, of course, all endings and beginnings were singular. They always were. I rubbed the back of my neck. I'd known that. Hadn't I? When I'd actually understood the workings of the universe. All right, I officially had Daniella in my head. I was going to go crazy if I wasn't careful with this. I had to be in control of myself.

Alexander took me in his arms. "Stay you, Aspen. Okay?"

I unfortunately understood exactly what he meant. "I will. I'm going to hold onto me."

He nodded at me like that was the answer he wanted. He lifted his chin, speaking to Reed. "Take care of our girl."

"With every ounce of my being."

Tears flooded my eyes. I didn't really know what I had done to earn the love of these five souls. Their devotion floored me. I had to be worth it. I wouldn't let them down.

"How does this work?" Jamie took my hands in his, kissing my knuckles. "Do you leave here? When you traveled into the past, you were here, but your mind was elsewhere."

That made sense. "I think I'll stay right here again. Reed and I—presuming I can figure out how to bring him with me —will go on a journey and see where this Darkness resides. Then we'll figure out what to do from there."

Jamie stepped back. "Good travels, my love. Thanks, Reed, for keeping her safe. It's good to have you back. For all of us to be back here together like this. It feels like right this second is what it always should have been like. I'm getting the impression that divinity held a bunch of cards back and didn't tell us everything we needed to know. Why they didn't have you tell us in the first place that you're the Warrior? Look at us. We've got it together. We're fine with the idea. We had no chance to react properly. Instead, they set us up for failure."

I touched his arm. "There will be time for answers, I hope. And I think it is always about choice. We can tell the whole world to be damned if we want to, but we choose not to. Divinity set us up and we chose a path. I bet there were others. Maybe they knew which one we'd likely do. I don't know. Even with all this power, I know nothing."

Reed held out his hand. "Let's do this thing."

I was ready.

❊ 1 2 ❊

I didn't know what I expected when I turned on my Oracle powers, but a dark winding road that looked like it should be in the middle of the woods wasn't anywhere on my map of possibilities. Reed stood next to me. I was glad he was with me, and I wasn't certain how I'd managed to bring him along.

If the Sisters were going to do this they should have left me written descriptions on how to operate their various talents. I could have had Stone read it to me.

I chewed on my bottom lip. I was doing this so often that if I wasn't careful, I was going to make myself bleed. "I want to learn how to read." I realized this wasn't all pressing at the moment, but it did keep weighing on my mind. "I'm only minimally competent."

Reed nodded. "Okay. That'll be what we do next after this. I want to learn how to cook. Or at least be able to make coffee. That was bad this morning, wasn't it?"

"Pretty horrible, actually."

He squeezed my fingers. "Now, if we're not careful you're going to follow this road to the most recently born Sister.

That's pretty much what Mika did. Or didn't do as the case may be since she downright refused the job sometimes."

"You're so in on the gossip, Reed. Flying around up there. Did you just listen to them all talk and complain most of the time?"

His smile was fast. "You might be surprised. Matchmaker. Peacemaker. Scapegoat. Gossip Monger. Yes, all me."

"Jamie was right. It is nice to be back, all of us together. I missed it more than I let myself feel."

I had to channel Teagan's power into Mika's power which meant that I was going to have to pull out some Daniella to do it. As though they were all recipes. "I can cook."

"Good. I'll teach you to read, you teach me to cook. Then we can get naked, fuck in the kitchen, and read a book after."

I snorted. I'd never have expected that from Reed. Alexander, yes. Reed, no. His eyes twinkled in the dark light of the road. "We could also drizzle ingredients on ourselves and read about sex."

"Sounds like a plan." He stopped walking. "Seriously, I'd stay here with you all day making sexual jokes and then actually complete the act on this walkway, but I think we have to get this done. But before we lose track and forget what we're supposed to be doing, I need to know if you can do this? It's fine if you can't. We'll find another way. Beelzebub was a low moment. He wanted to push at you so you'd know he was still Alpha demon. He did that. But it's neither here nor there. You weren't brought to this place to defeat him."

With his words in mind, I closed off my thoughts and centered myself. I drew Teagan and Daniella's powers to me. They tasted different. Like mint leaves and lavender. I could even smell the difference. Funny how a taste or a scent could so easily bring a person or place to mind.

I focused on the Darkness. I pictured him as last I'd seen him, the redheaded man. And the path changed. It moved, shifted, the horizon altered. I stared down at my feet. "Should we walk the new road?"

"I think that sounds like the right move."

Holding his hand, we traveled down the new path. Eventually, we came to a stop outside of a town. It was hard to make anything out clearly, but the need to go farther compelled me to keep walking. A pounding started in the back of my head, a drum beat looking for a rhythm.

When I hit the pinnacle of the noise, I stopped moving. There he was. By a lake, surrounded by possessed humans, souls who used to be alive but weren't anymore, their very essences being sucked away by the demon.

Like Krystal had said, he once again had red hair.

"That him?" Reed jerked his head toward the man.

I nodded. "That's him."

"Do we know where he is?"

I didn't want to move just then. "Could you go look for a sign? Anything that could tip us off? We have to be in walking distance of the Sisterhood. He's visiting us over there and there aren't any trains anymore. He's bringing hordes of demons with him. That means walking distance since I think we'd know if he was using a huge amount of carriages." I might have been rambling, but I hoped he understood.

Reed nodded. "On it."

He'd figure something out for me. As it was, I watched the Darkness. From before I was born, I'd been fated to meet this man. Beelzebub had been right. He was just a man. A fallen man who still wielded power. Guards were human. It was the Sisters who carried power. It was why the guards had to go sleep when they co-joined us. Their brains had to be reworked to fit ours.

This man—this person who had once been mortal—had done detestable things. I'd witnessed two of them in the several minutes I'd been watching. But he was human.

I supposed it made sense. We really were only guardians of humanity. It was their destiny that had to rise or fall. I would do the best I could, but it wasn't demons who brought them down in the end, it was one of their own.

I'd been one of their own, too. And maybe that was why, as much as I could hate him for what he'd done, I could also look at him and with a rising sadness filling my soul. How sad an ending for this man. He'd been chosen to be a guard. That meant someone like my Reed had thought his soul was worthy.

How truly pitiable to be brought so low.

He whirled around, his eyes glowing. Darkness couldn't see me. That much I knew, but he felt something. He sniffed the air like a dog. Did power have a scent?

"Are you there?"

I stepped closer to him, drawing my clothes tighter around myself. I couldn't feel the ground beneath my feet. I wasn't really physically present here. Still, I sniffed the air. Did evil have a scent?

We were practically nose-to-nose. "You'll never beat me. Your time has come to an end. I killed Krystal, and I'll take every one of you out."

So he didn't know. That was good. In this case, what he hadn't yet discovered was going to kill him.

Reed ran back to me. He grabbed my arm. "Not so close. I don't like it. Risky."

"Any luck?"

"Not yet. I've traveled the world fifty times over. This just looks like a nondescript town. It could be any number of places in the vicinity. We might spend a week looking."

Well, that wasn't going to do. Not in the least. "I don't need to know where he is."

"Why not? I'm getting nothing through our link. I feel determination but that's it. What have you decided?"

I put my hand on Reed's arm. "To win."

With a small tug, I returned us to the real world.

Reed met my gaze and shook his head. He didn't understand my plans and that was fine. I hadn't vocalized them, and much as I loved sharing my consciousness with my five loves, some things had to be kept private. This was one of them. They couldn't do this for me.

It had always been set up to be a battle for just two people.

And I would not risk my loves seeing me die.

"I think I might be hungry." I glanced up at Alexander. He'd wanted to feed me early. I wasn't actually in need of food, but it would make them happy to feed me and then we could talk. Hard conversations went better with full bellies. I'd heard that somewhere.

Gage took my hand, helping me up. "Did you find what you needed?"

"No," Reed said just as I answered the opposite. "Yes."

My One glared at me. "She's being tight mouthed about it."

"I realized as I stood there staring at him that I don't need him to be anywhere in particular. We're both going to battle, but it won't be here, there, or anywhere, per se. It will all take place as it was meant to be, in the other dimension. He crawls on walls, and I disintegrate. I don't think that location matters. It won't be solid; it will be everywhere." I walked toward the guesthouse. The main house was gone, so the smaller kitchen would have to do. "How about that food?"

They stayed where they were.

"What?" Stone yelled after me, hurrying to catch up. "What does that mean?"

"When she fights," Gage answered, "sometimes she vanishes. That's what she means. She's going to fight him like that and they don't even have to be in the same location."

Gage had understood perfectly.

"Jamie, you were right earlier. I love all of us being together again. It just works, you know?"

"She's changing the subject." Jamie laughed. "And using me to do it. Not okay."

I sighed. "Like it or not, if this fight happened, it happened this way. I knew it as I stood there looking at him in the other space. It is him and me. His demons won't be there, and much as I hate the idea, neither will you guys."

Alexander shook his head. "We're always there to help you in whatever ways we can. That's how this works."

I got up on my tiptoes to put my hands on his shoulders. "The way it works this time is that you kiss me goodbye and you tell me you love me. And then you hope that I do this and when I do you see me on the other side."

"I don't agree to those terms." Alexander shook his head. "No."

I reached up farther and kissed him. "You know the Sister motto? From the darkness to the light? How Anne had to do whatever she did and came out the other side? Teagan? Mika? This is mine. My battle is my darkness. And then we see if I can come out the other side in the light. Darkness to light. In this case, I'm actually fighting the darkness." I smirked. "Look at that word play."

"You're adorable, but it's not the time." Stone slammed his hand on the outside of the building. That had to hurt. I winced for him.

"Stone, you were thinking you might kill him for me?"

He didn't deny my guess and that made me love him even more. "I thought we could have tonight, but I think that might be making things harder. Kiss me, guys. Or don't if you can't. I can feel your love for me. That's all I need. All I have ever needed."

"You're going right now." Reed ran a hand through his hair. "Because you know that we can't really stop you, but we'll do everything to talk you out of this. And it's too late. It was too late the second Teagan transferred her powers. It took all choices away."

He stormed to me, his eyes glowing with heat. I didn't know that I'd ever seen Reed this intense before, and I would have said that I'd seen him very worked up on more than one occasion. I just didn't know how much more alpha he could be.

"This is all about choice. The Darkness chose. Well, you can, too. This is what you want? Because maybe I haven't made myself clear, and I'll do so right now. I love you. I would run away and watch the end of the world with you. And I will stand behind you while you battle. But what I don't want is for you to disappear and to never know what happened to you. That seems like... hell."

I leaned up to kiss him—hard. "I can feel it pulling on me, Reed. Like my powers turning on, I don't think I can say no. Maybe you're right. Maybe there was no choice ever. Maybe there was just this. But in any case I'll always be grateful that kismet brought me to you." I stepped back. "To all of you."

I think they must have felt it then, the futility of continuing this argument.

Jamie put his hand on my cheek. "You have to come back to us. And then we're going to yell at you for leaving us behind but only because we love you so much and you're scaring us."

I couldn't feel their fear. Had I shut down the link and didn't know it? I was so not in control of myself. Reed was right. This whole thing had taken away my choices. I could keep railing against that or I could get to work.

I kissed Jamie square on the lips. "I am going to do everything I can do to come back. I promise."

He nodded and stepped back. Gage tugged me into a strong hug. "I feel like this is my fault. I should have left you alone. You wouldn't be doing this now. I was missing you. I was selfish."

"This isn't about you. I'm glad you did what you did. I'd never trade this time for anything in the world."

He sucked in a breath before pulling back to kiss me. His tongue pressed against my mouth, and I opened it so he could make love to me tongue-to-tongue. For a second, we could both pretend everything was fine.

Gage finally released me to Stone. His poor burned face. I wished that had never happened to him. He narrowed his eyes at me. "I actually get this. You can't leave it. I couldn't either. But you aren't allowed to die because whatever nonsense about you disappearing or whatever is happening. I'm going to follow you wherever you go. There's no place you could go where I would not follow you."

I understood the implication. Even into nothingness. I was fully aware of what was at stake here.

He kissed me gently, and I rubbed the back of his neck. I wanted to melt into him. If only there was the time.

Stone finally let me go. I sighed, not wanting to take my eyes off of any of them. There was only Reed left. I turned to him. He slowly shook his head. "This isn't how it's supposed to be, love. We're always supposed to be at your side."

"I know. But what goes the way it's supposed to go when it comes to us?" I kissed him before he could say anything else. Reed was never going to be okay with this, and I understood why. We were a team, and I had to go off on my own. We'd been apart for so long. It wasn't fair that I was leaving them.

And yet as my head started spinning, I knew I had no choice.

I was being called to destiny. The future was on my shoulders. And I couldn't resist my role. I carried the dreams and powers of every Sister who had come before me. Much as I wanted to stay here and be with them, my lot in life had never been to just have love and family.

Maybe I would someday know why.

My fingers tingled. My powers were on. It was time.

"Come find me at the beach."

Alexander took an audible breath. "We'll find you wherever you are. Always."

I knew they would. They'd manipulated time and destiny for me. In the course of existence, there had never been five people more deserving of love and admiration than them. My guys. My guards. My everything.

I had to remake existence for them and so that was what I would do.

❦

THE PURPLE SUN BEAT DOWN ON MY HEAD, AND I REALIZED I was in the space I would always think of as divinity. Perhaps that was a misnomer because in reality, it was just another place. Divinity was everywhere, at least as far as I understood. There were all kinds of powers out there. If Krystal's journey had taught me anything, it was that.

I looked around. This place had been filled with people when last I was here and now it was empty. Even Sister Superior was missing from view. I truly was to do this alone.

I saw him standing ahead of me. He looked as he had in the past, redheaded, serious, and angry. Had there ever been a person as mad as he was?

"I see neither one of us was given a choice. We meet today, and we put an end to it."

I nodded. Had he battled the pull to come here as I had? Maybe the powers that be were simply sick of waiting for us to get around to it. Perhaps we were overdue. My own time-line hadn't mattered much in this war.

"Can I ask you a question?"

He smirked at me. "Sure. I'm going to kill you in a minute. You can ask me something first."

"I'm not afraid of death." As I said the words, I realized I meant them. I really wasn't. I didn't want my guys to suffer from emotional pain if I died, but other than that, I wasn't afraid of death. It eventually came to everyone. Now, if something came later that I wouldn't get to experience, that was sad but not enough to make me fear him. "What is your name? Your real name? I'm tired of calling you the Darkness."

He cocked his head to the side. He was obviously not prepared for that question. "It's been a long time since I used it or heard it. My mind stuttered trying to come up with it. But, Aspen." He clearly wanted to use my name to show he could. I didn't flinch. What did it matter? He could call me anything he wanted. "My name is Joseph. Or was. I am beyond needing a name."

The arrogance was worthy of eye rolling. I managed not to give in to the urge. It would help nothing, and I didn't need to have any more not so witty remarks from this man. The thought jarred me. Beelzebub had said it to me, and I hadn't really registered it earlier. This being in front of me was just a man.

"How did you do what you've done? How did you come back? You're human. You're not a demon. And yet you're possessing people."

He shrugged. "I may have convinced some demons to give me their powers. You might be surprised how easily people might give up their own power for the belief of something beyond themselves. Armageddon is what the demons want."

Joseph couldn't know just how much that resonated with me. I myself was deeply familiar with this concept. We really were two sides of the same coin.

He was sent to hell, and he came back as strong as a demon. The man must have some serious charisma I wasn't seeing.

"I see." I took a step to the side. "Shall we do this?"

"Let's."

He snapped his fingers and heat hit my body like I'd been thrown into the sun. The surprise of it made me cry out but only for a second. That was a neat trick but it was all that it was. A demonic maneuvering from some ridiculous demon who'd thought the best thing he could do was get into the proverbial bed with Joseph. I wasn't impressed.

A Sister had given me the know how to fix this. I cooled down, shedding his magic like a lizard might take off his skin. It would not hurt me.

"You're talented."

He had no idea. We pushed at the same time, both of us turning into nothing but cells. His evil pressed at me. I had no mouth, yet I could taste the acrid sense of him on my tongue. We rolled around in eternity. I shot him with energy, and he rounded on me. We were equally matched so this would come down to which of us tired first.

My mind twisted. Images, not of my life but of his, infected my brain. I didn't want to see his mother. I didn't want to know what he used to like to eat for dinner. I could have done without digesting his need for power and his frustration at being just a cog in the machine that was the guard network. He had never understood the love.

He felt no remorse.

His soul was distorted.

I didn't know what would happen if I did beat him. Would he return to hell and just do this again? Were we in an endless loop? Where we would never be rid of someone whose craving to feel important led him to destroy everything?

If I could be permanently nothing, then so damn it could he.

A vision of Krystal filled my mind. What had she said to me on the train? Why was I thinking about that now? Anne and I had bookended each other. We had both saved babies. We had both had to deal with the trains. We had...

That was right... I couldn't think in complete thoughts, just images as I battled.

I could see Anne as I'd last seen her, standing over me, giving me her powers that had brought back life to my body when it wasn't going to make it. That had been her gift. I had that gift.

I pushed at Joseph until he had to take his human form again. He snarled at me, his eyes turning red. That was the demon in him.

I grabbed onto him, and although it was the last thing I ever wanted to do, I pressed my lips to his, and I let Anne's power surge through me. She had the ability to bring on life. I pressed all of mine into his. He could only do what he did because he was dead—a soul that used powers not his own and created havoc in the world. He would live again.

I could see when Anne had done this. I could feel it around me. She'd discovered this power when she'd saved Bryant. She loved him. She gave him back his life. I did not love this man, just the opposite. I loved my guys. I loved the world. I wanted this over.

His eyes widened, the demon powers fleeing his body. He fell back onto his rear end.

He pounded on the ground. "You only think that stopped

me. I'll do it again. I'll go back to that hot, hellish existence, and I'll do it again. You watch. You can't stop me."

Oh, but I could. With my hands shaking, I knew I didn't have much time. I'd used so much power, but even with the huge amount that I had, it was too much.

I smiled down at him. Only I could beat him because I'd been human, because I had within me the grace bestowed only to humans from divinity. The Sisterhood of it. The joy that came from Darkness to Light. The way that humans could love each other and the humanity they could lay down for each other's survival.

Joseph wasn't going to hell; where he was going he could never hurt anyone else again.

"I forgive you."

❧ 13 ❧

He had to be ended. That was what was left to do. I stumbled forward, energy leaving me. I couldn't be done. Not until I killed him. It was a terrible thought, and yet I felt no sorrow at having to do this task.

A hand touched my arm, stopping me. Sister Superior stood next to me. "Aspen, thank you. That is enough. The rest is for others."

"You," Joseph cried out, curling into himself. I didn't understand. Was he scared of Sister Superior? He had certainly not seemed so earlier.

A veil lifted from my vision, and I could see the Sister. Not as she was now but as she was then—when she'd been his Sister and he'd killed her.

"No. No. I can't see you. I don't want to."

Maybe he wasn't as remorseless as he'd seemed. I sunk to my knees. I couldn't sustain my weight anymore. My life seemed to be fading from me, and I didn't have Anne to give it back. Still, I couldn't take my gaze off of what I witnessed. She walked toward him.

"You didn't get old. I'm sorry. I'm sorry that I failed you."

She bent over toward him. "I loved you, but it wasn't what you needed. It wasn't enough."

He sucked in a breath. "Why do I feel like this?"

"Because you were forgiven."

He blinked out of existence in her hands as she touched his shoulders. Her own slumped forward before she righted herself. I had to find my voice even though it didn't want to work. "Did it always have to be like this? Did you take my powers so that I'd be able to do this? Did you set this up?"

She walked toward me, bending down to embrace me in a hug. She smelled familiar, like I'd known her forever but hadn't seen her in just as long. "Yes, I did. I couldn't know. If you walked to the fountain right now and looked, if you spent more than one lifetime looking, you'd see how many things had to happen for this to occur. There are futures where he never killed me. I had to hope you could fix things and you did. All of you did."

All of us? She turned me enough that I could see my five guys behind me. They were here? A second later they were around me.

"We were here the whole time." Reed whispered in my ear. "Couldn't get to you but we were here. Had a little divine help. I may have pissed her off to no end, but she apparently has a soft spot for me."

"A guard who would do anything for his Sister? Even offer up his own life? I'm devoted to soul mates. You have no idea how much. Maybe it's obvious why now."

I shook in their arms. "I'm disappearing."

"You won." Alexander held me tighter. "You're not."

Sister Superior crossed to the fountain. "You are losing the powers that aren't yours. They're returning to their rightful owners."

"What happens now?"

Jamie stroked my hair in long swipes. "Now you get some sleep, Aspen. You don't have to be the Warrior anymore."

⁓⁂⁓

I WOKE UP TO THE SOUND OF THE OCEAN. MY HEAD WAS IN Stone's lap, my body resting comfortably on a towel over the sand. The sun was going down in the sky. The horizon was orange and red. "Here she is." Stone kissed my cheek as they all surrounded me. "I told you that she'd wake up soon."

I rubbed my eyes. "How long have I been asleep?"

"A long time. More than you'd want to know." Gage rubbed my arm. "And also not very long. Several hours."

"That doesn't make sense." I sat up slowly, letting the world right itself. "We're at the beach."

Reed handed me a glass of water, and I drank it down just as a noise caught my attention. In the sky, a large metal device shot through the atmosphere, leaving a trail of white clouds behind it.

I caught my breath. "What is that?"

Alexander squeezed my hand. "Search your memory. You've been given all the tools you need to live here, including what things are."

"What is here?" *It was an airplane. It took people long distances in short times by flying through the air like a bird.*

"The future." Jamie grinned at me. "We had to pick a time. You weren't available to discuss it, so we picked it for you. Hope that's okay. We thought you might like to see how well things turned out. Thanks to you it was not the end of days. Rather, a new beginning that led to this."

Reed kissed my cheek. "But if you don't like this, I bet they'd move you back. I mean, we're trying it out. We have a place to live and skills to get jobs. You can relax for a while. There is electricity everywhere. Air conditioning. And no demons. People live as they like. Small marriages, large ones. It's beautiful."

"We're all just human now." Gage delivered the information as though he worried I wouldn't like it.

I sucked in a long breath. For someone who had wanted to be a Sister my whole life, I hadn't appreciated the loveliness of being human when I'd had it. Now? I never wanted to be anything else. "As long as we can all be together, I don't care if we live in a tin can in some time I've never heard of."

Stone breathed into the back of my neck. "You saved the world, baby. I think we can do a lot better than that."

I almost asked about the others, and then I didn't. It wasn't necessary. I might have been human now, but divinity granted me one last wish: to see the Sisters who had saved my life and made the ultimate sacrifices so this place could exist.

Teagan... she'd been the first. She smiled and laughed, her daughter on her hip as she walked toward her husbands. The town she was in was modern. A car drove by her. She turned like she was looking at me and winked.

"I knew you'd do it, Aspen. We're not far from each other. We'll see each other again. I believe that."

I gasped as she faded away. The scene changed. Mika. She walked toward the ocean, but it wasn't here. No, a carriage caught my attention. She hadn't left the time we'd lived in. Her husbands had come from a lovely sounding place. I'd bet she was back there.

She grinned as she walked. "Hey there, Aspen. Welcome back. You slept a long time. Been waiting for you to check in. I'm well. Good work. I don't know if I'd have thought about that. We're in a different time. I wish you only the best and the same happiness I have here. I'm rebuilding. We're going to get this place set up so someday it can be what you have."

I wanted to answer her, but I couldn't because in the next moment I was with Krystal. She stretched out on top of a mountain. She was dressed in warm clothes, a glass of what looked like steaming liquid in her hands. "I knew you'd do it. Even if I broke some rules helping. When am I? Well, between you and Mika. How's that?" A toddler ran to her, and she scooped him up. "I get to live again. A brand new life. No death. No rebirths. One life now. That's for all of us."

She floated away, and staring at me as she stood in front of a rebuilt Sisterhood was Daniella. Students dressed in uniforms ran behind her. "What I really loved doing was teaching. We rebuilt this place and that is what we're doing now. I'll open minds to all kinds of ideas. I'm happy. Be happy, Aspen. You more than earned it. What a remarkable thing you did. Bravo."

Her words were beautiful. They brought tears to my eyes. She disappeared in a cloud, and in her place Anne stood, a purple sun beating down on her. She wore Sister robes, and her smile was huge. Had she become the true Sister Superior?

She reached her hand to me, and I could feel it. "It's my turn now." Her sons and daughter ran around her. "We're here. If you need us. If the world needs us, we'll call on you, on the others with hearts like yours. For now, enjoy your life, you lovely woman. You more than earned it, and you'll always be our Warrior. Keep an eye out for Bob. He's around in every time. He sometimes causes small annoyances. Love you."

It all faded away. For a second, it was hard to believe that any of this had happened. They were all content, every Sister I could touch with my mind had found and earned happiness. I got to my feet. "Well, I think there is a thing called pizza that I know about but haven't tried. Let's go find it."

All it had taken to be here with my loves were women willing to balk at tradition, overcome the past, rewrite their destinies, show compassion when others would flee, and tell the future it would be of their own making.

I was so glad to have been a part of it.

Reed scooped me up. "Pizza it is."

"Oh, do you think they have pineapple?" Alexander sounded giddy.

"On your pizza? Blah?" Stone was less than thrilled.

I laughed. This was all I wanted. All of us together. Always. The rest of the world could be damned. Or maybe not. No, I didn't want that. We'd just won that battle. The rest of the world needed to find its own happiness, and I had to believe it would. Some of the most amazing women I'd ever had the privilege to know invested their passion to flout tradition, to avert destiny, rediscover compassion and ensure a future where our guards and we could live and love in peace. We did it for the rest of the world, for all time.

Now, we lived for each other and our happily ever afters.

Mine started right here on this beach—with my soulmates.

Future be blessed.

AFTERWORD

Thank you so much for reading the *Last Hope* series. I hope that you liked the five book journey from Tradition to Future. I loved writing it. If you have a minute, I'd appreciate it if you could leave a quick review of the book. Reviews go a long way to help Indie authors. Now, I'm also hoping I can convince you to try some more of my writing while I have you here. I have over 80 books published. Do you like reverse harem novels? I have a very exciting science fiction romance, reverse harem series called Wings of Artemis. The whole series is on Kindle Unlimited. You can find the first book here: https://amzn.to/2Nao51H

Also, I have a readers group on Facebook that I visit every day to ask my readers random questions and talk about books! The group is called Rebecca's Randomness and I'd love it if you would come and join. You can find it here: https://bit.ly/2N4ZePv

Please turn the page for a complete list of all of my books. Hope to see you again soon. –Rebecca Royce

ABOUT THE AUTHOR

As a teenager, I would hide in my room to read my favorite romance novels when I was supposed to be doing my homework. I hope, these days, that my parents think it was worth it.

I am the mother of three adorable boys and I am fortunate to be married to my best friend. I live in Austin Texas where I am determined to eat all the barbecue in town.

I am in love with science fiction, fantasy, and the paranormal and try to use all of these elements in my writing. I've been told I'm a little bloodthirsty so I hope that when you read my work you'll enjoy the action packed ride that always ends in romance. I love to write series because I love to see characters develop over time and it always makes me happy to see my favorite characters make guest appearances in other books.

In my world anything is possible, anything can happen, and you should suspect that it will.

I'd love to hear from you! Please visit my website at www.rebeccaroyce.com to sign up for my newsletter and learn about my books!

Here's where you can find me online:
www.rebeccaroyce.com

Rebecca's Randomness Reading Group
https://bit.ly/2N4ZePv

www.twitter.com/rebeccaroyce

Instagram: rebeccaroyce79

Cheers!!
Rebecca

OTHER BOOKS BY REBECCA ROYCE...

Wings of Artemis

Kidnapped By Her Husbands

Rescued by Their Wife

Crashing Into Destiny

Meeting Them

Reclaiming Their Love

Loving Them

Ship Called Malice

Saving Them

Dark Demise

Light Unfolding

Still Waters (coming soon)

Last Hope (completed series)

Tradition Be Damned

Past Be Damned

Destiny Be Damned

Compassion Be Damned

Future Be Damned

Dragon Wars (completed series)

Forever

Eternal

Always

Evermore

Endless

Wards and Wands

Hexed and Vexed

Curse Reversed

Meow, Baby (novella, Coming Soon in Petting Them antho, co-written with Ripley Proserpina)

Tragic Magic (Coming Soon)

Safe Haven

Everywhere and Nowhere

Dimension X (coming soon)

More coming soon....

Soul Bound

Prisoner of the Dragons

More coming soon....

Shadow Promised

Strange Days

Weird Nights

Bizarre Years

More coming soon...

The Warrior (completed series)

Initiation

Driven

Subversive

Redemption

Justice

Warrior World (spin off of The Warrior, completed series)

Deacon

Micah

Jason

The Westervelt Wolves (completed series)

Her Wolf

Summer's Wolf

Wolf Reborn

Wolf's Valentine

Wolf's Magic

Alpha Wolf

Angel's Wolf

Darkest Wolf

Lone Wolf

Fallen Alpha

Alpha Rising

Alpha's Strength

Alpha's Sacrifice

Alpha's Truth

Alpha Enticing

Hidden Alpha (coming soon)

The Capes (completed series)

Seductive Powers

Adrenaline Rush

Last Ascension

The Conditioned

Eye Contact

Embraced

Unlawful (coming soon...)

The Outsiders

Love Beyond Time

Love Beyond Sanity

Love Beyond Loyalty

Love Beyond Sight

Love Beyond Expectations

Love Beyond Oceans

Love Beyond Flames

Love Beyond Lies (coming soon)

Cascade (completed series)

Haunted Redemption

Phoenix Everlasting

Fragility Unearthed

Persuasion Enraptured

Reverse Harem Story

Unconventional

Unexpected

Undeniable (Coming Soon)

www.ingramcontent.com/pod-product-compliance
Lightning Source LLC
Chambersburg PA
CBHW011456170626
46814CB00009B/3076